What kids say about *Everybody's Favorite...*

"This book is a kick in the goal. It teaches many valuable lessons in life."

–Jessica, 11

"I recommend this five-star, two thumbs-up book to a girl, any age."

–Clare, 11

"If I were stranded on a desert island and I had to have one of the Ballplayers help me escape, I would want Penny with me. She always puts other people before herself."

–Christopher, 12

"I do not play soccer, but I still loved this book. Athletes and non-athletes will be able to relate to Penny and her friends."

–Nora, 12

"I like how this book shows that even perfect people can make mistakes."

–Chrissy, 11

Other books by **The Broadway Ballplayers**™

Book 3

The Broadway Ballplayers™

To Miss Cohn,
Play and teach
with passion!
Maureen Holohan

Everybody's Favorite
by Penny

Series by
Maureen Holohan

For information regarding permission, please write to:

The Broadway Ballplayers, Inc.
P.O. Box 597
Wilmette, IL 60091
(847)-570-4715

ISBN: 0-9659091-2-3

*This book is dedicated
to those who treat all people
with dignity and respect.*

You make a difference.

Chapter One

The Real Deal. The Legend. Big Time.
That's what they called me.

When I heard these nicknames, I just shrugged and smiled. I was 12 years old, and I already knew that everybody expected me to be great. People wanted so badly for me to rise above everyone else that I had no other choice but to try and do just that. When the game was on the line, I had to score. When the teacher called on me in school, I had to be right. It was as if the clock was always running. There were no time-outs, and there was no such thing as starting over.

Or so I thought. One summer, with the pressure on me like never before, I learned something else. Here's how it all began.

• • • •

My six year-old brother, Sammy, bounced the basketball with his right hand while his tiny, quick feet moved smoothly over the asphalt.

Angel smiled at him, and called out, "Pass it!" When Sammy kept running with a big grin on his face, Angel groaned.

Then Rosie tried sneaking up behind him. He giggled as he safely scooted away.

Wil rested her hand on her hip as she stood under the basket, and shouted, "Shoot the darn ball, Sammy!"

I laughed. There was nothing else in the world quite like playing ball with my friends at our favorite hangout. The two basketball courts, set of swings, and open playing field might have seemed like a plain old park in any city. But to the kids from Broadway Ave., Anderson Park was *our* park in *our* city.

"Let's play a game," Sammy said.

"We're playing a game," I said.

"No," he said, "a real game."

"You're not playing if we do," Wil said.

"Why not?"

"Because you're a shorty," Wil said. "You've got to wait 'til you're bigger."

Sammy's big droopy eyes turned toward me, "Why can't I, Penny?" he asked. "That's not fair."

"Wait until next summer," I said. "Then it will be OK."

It was enough of a promise to get him through the moment. He tossed the ball up in the air and Angel grabbed the rebound.

"Hey!" a voice called out.

I turned and watched my best friend, Molly O'Malley, jog toward us. With a basketball tucked under her right arm and a crumbled piece of paper in her left hand, Molly kept jogging until she reached us on the courts.

"Let's jump in the double-Dutch competition!" she called out.

"What competition?" Angel asked while Molly panted for air.

"The one at the Summer Fest," Molly said. She handed the piece of paper to Angel. "Look. It's in three weeks."

While Angel and Rosie read the flyer, I glanced over at Wil. She arched her eyebrows, and I rolled my eyes. We always got a kick out of Molly's wild ideas, but this one was too much.

"Molly," I said, "you don't know how to jump."

Her blue eyes grew bright. "You can teach me!"

I took a deep breath and smiled. *She can't be serious.*

Angel asked, "Can you even skip one rope?"

Everyone laughed except for Molly. "Come on," she pleaded. "We're the *Ballplayers.*"

"Ballplayers play ball, not jump rope," I explained.

"It's a neighborhood thing," she argued. "We gotta do it."

She had a point. Ever since our team had played in a city basketball league that summer, we were no longer just the kids from Broadway. We were the Ballplayers. The Broadway Ballplayers. Our tight group of friends — Molly, Wil, Angel, Rosie and me — always stuck together. It was an unwritten pact and an unspoken promise between all of us.

I took a deep breath. "All right," I said. "I'm in."

"Anyone else?" Molly asked. "We need one more to make a team."

"I'd do it," Angel said, "but I may have cross-country practice."

"When will you know for sure?" Molly asked.

"I don't know," Angel said as she tightened the purple bow in her hair. "I'll be around to help out when I can."

At the end of August, Angel Russomano would be going into high school. Between cross-country running and soccer, our oldest friend would soon have little time for anything else. Our attention turned to Rosie Jones, whose baseball cap held down her long braid of thick brown hair.

"I may have a tournament," Rosie said. She was one of the best baseball players in the city. "Sorry, Molly."

It came down to one last person. Molly and I both turned to Wil, hoping that she would be faithful.

"Oh, no," Wil groaned and she shook her head. "Do you know how much we'll have to practice just to be able to *compete?* Those girls are *good.* "

"We're not gonna lose," Molly shot back confidently. "Trust me."

"Yeah, right," Wil said. "I'm gonna trust a girl who trips when she tries to jump over a crack in the sidewalk."

"We gotta do this," Molly pleaded. "It will be fun."

Wil looked at her, burst out laughing, and then turned to the rest of us. "She's nuts," she said shaking her head. "This is the biggest party of the summer! Everybody will be there."

"Come on, Wil," Molly insisted. "Please?"

Wil picked the basketball up off the ground. She dribbled with one hand while the other pulled her long T-shirt over her tight shorts. After she shot the ball, her glasses slid down her nose and she pushed them up with her middle finger. Even though she was only entering the eighth grade, I was convinced that Wilma Thomas had to be the brightest person who ever lived on Broadway Ave. She never received anything less than an A. Not even one A-.

"No, Molly," Wil replied. "No way."

"Thanks a lot," Molly muttered sarcastically. "You're a real friend."

As the ball bounced up and down on the pavement, no one said a word. Molly looked at me and scoffed. It was her way of asking for my help.

"How much money can we win?" I asked.

"Fifty bucks," Molly said.

Wil stopped and stared up into the sky. "That's 16 dollars and 60 cents a person," she quickly calculated. Then she turned to us. "I'd like the full 17 dollars if we win."

"*When* we win," Molly corrected her.

"Fine," Wil said. "*When* we win."

Chapter Two

For almost three weeks, Molly tripped and tangled herself up every time she tried to jump. While everyone took turns rolling their eyes and shaking their heads, I kept taking deep breaths and trying to smile for one simple reason. I was the one who had agreed to teach Molly.

"I just don't know, Penny," Wil whispered to me one day. "I just don't know if it's possible."

"She can do it," I assured Wil.

"You really think she can, Penny?" Wil asked.

"Yeah," I said.

"What?" Wil exclaimed. "Would you look at her feet! She's jumping all over the place. She's too fast, then she's too slow. She's a spaz, Penny. She really is."

Wil wasn't exactly the queen of coordination herself, but I could see where she was coming from. I watched as Molly's heavy and clumsy feet pounded the pavement. She was definitely moving to a beat I had never quite seen before.

"Give her some time," I replied calmly.

"What?" Wil gasped. "We're talking eternity here, P. And I'm really not in the mood to humiliate myself or my friends at the biggest party of the summer."

"Keep your cool," I assured Wil.

I always banked on one last thing when all else failed — luck. My grandmother, who nicknamed me Penny so I would have a little luck with me all the time, always told me that lucky things just don't happen by themselves. She said the only way I'd ever have any luck in life was if I never let go of hope.

In this case, believing that my best friend would pull through was not hard for one reason. Molly O'Malley worked harder and longer than any person I'd ever met. When coaches told Molly to practice three times a week, Molly practiced twice a day. When we were told to run a mile in gym class, she always ran two. On the days when her jump-rope skills were really shaky, I continued to believe. I had to. Molly and Wil were my friends, and we were all in this together.

But time was running out. There we were, less than 24 hours away from the competition, and we still had a potential disaster on our hands. Just when everyone else thought we should tie up our rope and go home, Molly called out for one more try.

"Please?" Molly pleaded.

"This is it," Wil said. "Just one more time, and we're done."

I glanced at my best friend. I could tell by Molly's glassy eyes and red face that she was ready to cry.

"You can do it," I told her. "Don't give up."

She nodded, and I held my breath. Angel and Wil started the ropes. Molly pushed off the pavement and entered cleanly. Then she started to really move. Our grins grew wide as Molly's striped green sneakers continued to spring up and down on the blacktop.

"Work it...work it..." Wil bellowed while her arms twirled the ropes.

"You got it!" Angel added from her end. "You're doing it, Molly!"

I turned to Rosie, who had been standing next to me lazily slapping her baseball in and out of her mitt. She stopped and her mouth dropped open.

"Yeah, Molly!" Rosie cheered.

"Yeah!" I called out. "You go!"

What was happening right before our eyes was easily one of the most amazing things that ever happened at Anderson Park.

Molly O'Malley had finally discovered rhythm.

"Don't stop now!" Wil said. "Keep it going. Keep it goin' now."

"I got it," Molly said between breaths. "I got *rhythm!*"

"You got it all right," Angel added with a laugh. "I never thought I'd see the day."

"I can't believe it," said Wil, who was still shaking her head. "I really can't believe it."

Just as Molly's smile grew wider, her right leg got caught up in one rope. She couldn't recover. The ropes came to a halt, and Molly's curly auburn pony tail stopped flipping back and forth.

"Ugh..." she moaned.

"All good things come to an end," Wil said and then she sighed.

"You had it, Molly," I said surely. "Shake it off. Don't get all down on yourself."

Not now. As much as we were supposed to get swept up in the simple joy of competition, everyone knew our reputation was on the line.

"What time does it start tomorrow?" Molly asked.

"Five," Wil reminded her.

"Can we come and practice again in the morning?" Molly begged.

"You're crazy," said Angel. "I volunteered our rope twirling time, but I don't work Saturday mornings. I'm sleeping in."

"Me, too," Rosie added.

"Don't worry, Molly," Angel said. Her voice was firm. "I know you can do it."

Molly took a deep breath and rested her hand on her hip. "I hope so," she mumbled.

"Hi girls," a deep voice called out. I looked over to a tall man pulling up on a navy mountain bike. He slipped off his shades and twisted them gently in his shirt. Our grade school principal, Mr. Gordon, was on one of his daily patrols of Anderson Park.

"Hey, Mr. G," I said.

"How's everybody doing?" he asked.

"Ask us tomorrow after the contest," Wil said.

"I can see you've been practicing a lot," he said.

It was no secret that Mr. G saw everything. It was as if he had security cameras hidden in the streetlights.

"I'm sure you'll do your best," he added.

I had never seen a person as loyal as Mr. Gordon. Unlike most of the teachers who never set foot in our homes, Mr. G went to dinner at students' homes sometimes two or three nights out of the week. And like it or not, every kid on Broadway Ave. knew that Mr. Gordon cared. One day when

15

Bobby Barton skipped school, Mr. Gordon left the building and went to his house. I know this because our entire social studies class was right behind him, waiting outside on the sidewalk. When Bobby came to the door, I stepped forward as Mr. G had asked, and told Bobby that we wanted him in school with us. Without a word, Bobby shook his head in disbelief and ducked back inside. Thirty seconds later, he came out in a shirt and jeans, and locked the door behind him. We all walked back to school together.

"Do you girls have anything planned next week?" Mr. Gordon asked.

We all shrugged. Nobody wanted to give him an answer until we knew what he had in mind.

"I just thought if you were getting bored and needed something to do," he said. "Idle hands are..."

"The devil's workshop," Wil finished.

"We know Mr. G," Angel said. "We know."

"We're not bored," Molly said with pride. "I just wish we were still playing basketball on Friday nights."

"I have something that you might be interested in," he said.

He pressed his lips together in a tight smile. All of us glanced eagerly up at him.

"Would you girls be interested in going to soccer camp?" he asked.

"Yeah," Angel said excitedly. "When?"

"It starts Wednesday," he said.

Within seconds, Mr. G was the only one talking. Molly's eyes dropped to the ground, and Wil took a deep breath. Rosie kept slapping her ball in and out of her mitt. Angel turned to me, and I asked the dreaded question.

"How much does it cost?"

"With a little bit of fundraising," he said, "You'll be able to go for free."

It was music to our ears. As the rest of us smiled in relief, Wil asked, "How much will we have to raise?"

"You'll each need $75," he said.

"By Wednesday?" Wil asked.

Mr. Gordon nodded. "And the only way you can go is if everyone can go."

Wil sighed loudly. "That's $375 in less than a week," she said.

"That's a lotta of money," Angel added.

"Now we have to win the jump rope competition," I said.

"How much can you win?" Mr. Gordon asked.

"Fifty dollars," Angel said.

"Even *when* we win," Molly said emphatically, "we're still gonna need more money."

"What about a bake sale?" Angel offered. "My aunt and some of her friends baked some cookies and cupcakes to raise money for my church last summer."

"There's an idea," Mr. Gordon added.

"We could sell them at the Summer Fest tomorrow," I said.

"Yeah," Molly replied. "We could set up our own booth."

"I can make some of my favorite double-fudge brownies," Wil added.

"Well," Mr. Gordon said as he looked at his watch. "It's almost seven. You might want to go on home and check what you've got in the cupboards."

"Do you wanna start at my house?" I asked my friends. "My grandma's there. She can help us get started."

"Sounds good," Wil said as she finished braiding the jump rope. We each yelled thanks to Mr. Gordon and took one last sip from the water fountain.

"I'll see you at the party tomorrow," he added as he rolled away on his bike. "Good luck in the competition. Be safe."

Together we walked up Woodside and then turned right down Broadway Ave. Coming right at us on the sidewalk were the regulars from our neighborhood — Eddie, J.J., Sleepy, Mike, and Billy Flanigan.

"Where you going?" J.J. asked as he picked up his basketball. "We just came down to play."

"We've got some business to take care of," Wil said coolly.

"Whatever that means," Eddie quipped, and then he laughed. "You too scared to play us?"

"Oh, *puh-leze!*" Wil said.

"Just admit it," Eddie said.

"Yeah, we're *real* scared," Angel mumbled sarcastically. "We're just resting to embarrass you on the courts at the party tomorrow."

Molly turned my way. "Just one game?" she asked.

"No," I said. "We gotta go."

"Just one?"

I took a deep breath. As much as we needed to go, none of us could stand walking away from a little competition.

"Fine," I said. "One and we're outta here."

It was the girls against boys, which wasn't something we normally did. But after Eddie insulted us by calling us scared, we had to remind them who they were dealing with. I checked the ball to J.J.

"Ball is in," I called out.

Molly grunted, pushed, and shoved her way through the first five minutes without scoring a basket, which made her more frustrated. Even though Wil was named after the track star Wilma Rudolph, unfortunately she never ran like the woman. But we could always count on her for rebounds. Every shot Angel put up that day fell short. Even though Rosie used her quick feet to play some serious defense, what we needed was offense.

So I took the game into my own hands. I shot and drove and wheeled and dealed. After falling behind by five baskets, I scored four in a row. Then I dished the ball to Molly. She scored a lay-up. Angel grabbed a rebound on the next play, and put it back in the basket. Then J.J. hit a jumpshot. With the score tied at 10-10, I had the ball in my hands again. I drove to the basket and sunk a left-handed lay-up off a spin move. On the next play, I grabbed Wil's rebound and banked it in.

"That's game!" Molly called out as she pumped her fist in the air.

Molly reveled in the glory of winning, especially when the boys were on the losing end. But it wasn't over. The trash-talking was just getting started.

"Slow as a turtle, that's what you are Molly," J.J. said.

"Shut up," Molly said.

"Breadloaf," J.J. muttered.

"Creampuff!" Molly shot back.

Powerful words like breadloaf and creampuff always entered the post-game jab session. Nothing was taken too seriously, unless it became personal.

"If you didn't have Penny," Eddie yelled to our group as we walked away. "You'd never win."

That was personal. Not one of my friends said a word. So many questions raced in my mind. *What are they thinking? Are they mad at me?*

"He's right," Wil muttered. "If it weren't for you, we'd never win."

"You always do everything for me," Molly said. "You do everything for everyone."

They were not just saying this; they were telling me as if it was something that I had to change. Suddenly I wasn't sure if they wanted me to do everything all the time. *Did they want me to shoot less? Or pass more? Did they want me to lose? Should I even care?*

"See you wimps tomorrow," Eddie called out. "We won't embarrass you too bad."

Molly turned around and screamed, "Get a haircut, Eddie!"

The burst of laughter wiped all the pressure away. I breathed a quiet sigh of relief and gladly joined the conversation with my friends.

"They're going to be so mad when they hear we're going to camp," Angel said.

"Yeah," I said. "But Mr. G sent them to basketball camp last month."

"They're still gonna be so jealous," Wil added.
We all grinned devilishly.

Chapter Three

As we walked down Broadway Ave., the questions about the bake sale started flying.

"Who's gonna cook what?" Molly said.

"Can I help?" Sammy asked as he looked up at me.

"I can make some brownies," Angel offered.

"I wanted to make the brownies," Wil whined.

"You always get to make the brownies," Molly said. "Why don't you let somebody else?"

Wil clicked her tongue, and said, "Fine."

Molly winced as she looked at Wil, and asked, "Why do you gotta be so sensitive?"

"I'm not," Wil shot back. "Go ahead, you make the brownies."

Molly and Wil enjoyed arguing over nothing sometimes, which became annoying.

"Relax," I said softly. "It's no big deal."

There was a brief pause and then Rosie asked, "What do you want me to do?"

All my friends turned to me. My mind raced for a solution that would please everyone.

"We'll make a list at my house," I said. "My grandma will help."

Passing the responsibility on to an adult worked only if the adult earned the approval of the group.

There were no objections here. My grandmother lived on the South Side, and on the weekends in the summer she stayed at our house. Molly and Wil told me they always knew when she was in to visit because they could smell her sweet potato pie from down the street. And even though Rosie's mother cooked up some tasty Puerto Rican dishes, Rosie said that she'd gladly stay for dinner any time my grandmother was cooking.

We walked up the sidewalk, skipped up the steps and walked into my house.

"I'll go tell grandma about the bake sale," Sammy said, and he ran off into the kitchen.

Within seconds, Sammy had delivered the news.

"A bake sale?" my grandma called out. "You girls come on in here."

As my friends and I filed into the kitchen, my grandmother turned from the sink. She took her glasses off of her nose and greeted us all with a wide smile.

"You have any sweet potato pie?" Wil asked.

"No," she answered. "But I'll be making some for the party tomorrow."

Wil grinned, and so did Molly.

"What's this about a bake sale?" my grandmother asked.

"We can go to soccer camp if we can raise enough money," I explained.

"And how much would that be?" she asked.

"Three hundred and seventy-five dollars," Wil replied.

Without the slightest change of expression, my grandmother said, "You girls have some cookin' to do."

After she slipped on her glasses, she went to the cupboard, and eyed the racks of baking goods. My grandmother could make just about anything from scratch. That's because most of her life, she had no other choice but to do the most with what little she had.

Although my grandmother had graduated at the top in her high school class and was offered a college scholarship, her father wouldn't let her go on with her education. When she told me that, I couldn't understand how anyone could have let that happen. She said things were different back then. Her family needed her to work on the farm, so she had no other choice but to do as she was told.

A few years after high school, she met my grandfather. They married and had six kids. But when he was just 35 years old, my grandfather was killed in a coal mine accident. I only knew him from the pictures I had seen. He had a soft, gentle smile, long curly eye lashes and light brown skin just like my brother. My grandmother said that he was the most gentle man she ever knew. My father never really said much about his father around Sammy and me. He just told us that he wouldn't have made it without his mother, who had worked three jobs and raised five boys and one girl all by herself. I heard that for years, my grandmother never had a plate of food for dinner. She just went around and ate what was left over from her kids' plates without one single complaint. As long as her kids were in school, she was happy.

"This bake sale will get you started," she said. "But you'd better be thinking of other ways to raise the money you need. Penny, grab a sheet of paper and pen."

I grabbed a piece of paper and a pen from the desk, and let my grandmother take over. She called out what we could bake, and then started assigning everyone else their responsibilities.

"Have your mother make those cupcakes," she said to Molly.

Wil added, "I can make my favorite brownies."

"Good," my grandma said and then she turned to Angel. "Darlin', can you make some Angel's food cake?"

"Sure," Angel said with a smile.

"And Little Miss Shy over there, how about some cookies?"

Rosie lifted her eyes up and nodded eagerly.

My grandma gave out some more instructions, and hustled us out of the kitchen.

• • • •

For three straight hours, my grandmother measured and mixed like a machine. I stood by her side and did as I was told. Everything was timed perfectly.

"Five more minutes and you're off to bed," she said. "You need your rest for tomorrow."

The front door opened, and in came my father with Sammy asleep in his arms. They had gone out for ice cream after dinner. My father carried my brother into my room, and gently set him down on my bed. No matter how many times we tried to trick Sammy into sleeping in his own room by himself, it never worked. If Sammy woke up in the middle of the night without me next to him, I would hear him whimpering through the wall that separated us. Within seconds of calling out for him, I'd hear a thud, then the tapping of his footsteps. Then I'd feel a tug on my sheet and the weight of one boy and a teddy bear next to me. I didn't mind too much, but I sometimes lay awake wondering how long it would be before Sammy could sleep alone.

My father had the responsibility of tucking us in because my mother worked the evening shift as a nurse in the emergency room. Just like Mrs. O'Malley, she came home around midnight. It was rare that we saw her before we went to bed.

The next morning, I felt the sunlight spill all over me from the window of my bedroom. Without looking, I knew it was my mother who had twisted open the blinds. I buried my head in my sheet and curled up into a ball.

"Good morning," she said. "You've got a big day ahead of you. I heard all about soccer camp and the bake sale. Make sure you and your friends thank Mr. Gordon."

My grandmother walked past my door, and as usual, she had her ears into everything. "He's always keeping you kids busy," my grandmother said approvingly. "Idle hands are the devil's workshop."

There it was again. That same saying Mr. Gordon had used the day before.

"Why does everybody have to say that around here?" I asked. "Do people expect us to get into trouble?"

"We just know what's out there," my mother said. "And we want you to be safe."

That didn't really answer my question of what was expected of us, but I let it go. My mother just kept talking until my body was wide awake. I walked into the kitchen, and sat down at the table for some breakfast. When I finished, I went into the living room, curled up into a ball on the couch, and watched television. I could hear my mother and grandmother fussing around in the kitchen getting ready for the party. The aroma of the sweet potato pie drifted into the living room.

"You better get yourself together, Penny," my grandmother called out. "We're leaving in a couple of hours."

The Summer Fest was all afternoon and all night long. I didn't understand why we had to rush to get there.

"You've got some money to raise," my grandmother added.

Then my mother said, "Penny, please get out the vacuum and run it across the living room."

"I've got some dishes here in the sink, too," my grandmother added.

In a minute. In a minute. They were always bugging me about keeping up with my chores, and helping them with errands. I wanted to tell them both that I was busy watching television, but I didn't say a word. If I did, they would have been all over my case about being lazy and having a bad attitude. It was too early in the morning to hear a lecture, so I went straight to the closet, pulled out the vacuum and started my work. Just after I had finished vacuuming the rug, my father and brother came through the front door.

"Good morning!" my father said. He wiped the sweat off his forehead with the towel that rested on his shoulders. He had just finished a Saturday morning of basketball. "Do I have any volunteers to help me mow the lawn?"

Of course, my father was looking right at me.

"I just cleaned the house," I said.

"I didn't raise you just to do housework," he said. "Get your clothes on and come on outside." My shoulders drooped. Before I took on another responsibility, we needed to talk about compensation for my work.

"Only if I can get a raise in my allowance," I suggested.

"No raise until you can beat me in a game of one-on-one." He grinned proudly at his remark, knowing that wasn't about to happen any time soon. Even though my attempt at getting some extra funds fell by the wayside, I wasn't finished with him just yet.

"Your stomach is looking a little round there, Dad," I said.

"You mean my chest," he said as he pulled his shoulders back and sucked in his gut. "It's from lifting weights."

I laughed. As much as I enjoyed teasing him, I knew that he was no old man. He still had the moves that made him a basketball legend in the city. People assumed that I would be the next Harris to amaze them, too. All eyes were on me all the time when I was on the basketball court. I played and I had fun most of the time. But I didn't like it when people bet money on me, and called out my name in front of all my friends. Sometimes it was as if others wanted me to play just so they could have fun. I thought if I tried a different sport like soccer and softball, I'd get a break from all the attention. But I was good at those sports, too.

"Let's go, Penny," my dad said. "You've got to earn your keep."

"I gotta get ready for the party," I said as my little brother burst into the room behind my father.

"Just for a few minutes," he said. "You've got a lot of time."

I looked at my little brother, who was smiling and dancing around the living room. "How old do you have to be to earn your keep?" I asked my father.

"Let's go, little man," my dad said to my brother. "I'll find something for you to do, too."

After a morning of cleaning and trimming, we were almost ready to go. I spent 20 minutes hot-curling my hair, and fixing my headband so it would fit perfectly under my curls. My policy was that if you looked sloppy, you played sloppy. I tucked my shirt neatly into my shorts as I walked into the kitchen.

"Do you have to wear those bands all the time?" my grandmother asked. "You're going to a party, not playing ball."

"We'll end up playing," I said. "We always do."

Chapter Four

Everyone on the North Side of the city planned weeks ahead for the Summer Fest. I always wanted it to be held at Anderson Park, but our park wasn't big enough. Tucker Park's pavilion, three basketball courts, large wooden playground, two tennis courts, and two baseball fields provided more space, but not for long. As we slowly drove up to the parking lot, my eyes searched through the mobs of people.

"Where are we meeting the girls?" my dad asked.

"By the baseball field over there," I said as I pointed. "Behind the backstop."

He pulled into the closest spot by the baseball field. As I jumped out of the car, I saw Wil proudly hold her plate out.

"I made two pans of double-fudge brownies," she shouted.

"I have three dozen cupcakes, and only four dozen chocolate chip cookies," Molly said, grumbling. "My brothers ate the other dozen when I wasn't looking."

My father pulled the folding table out of the trunk and set it down. Angel and Rosie piled their tins and pans on top.

"Umm, Umm," my father said. "I'll take one of everything."

"How much do you think we should sell them for, Mr. H?" Molly asked.

Just as my father started calling out prices, my grandmother jumped in.

"That's not enough," she said. "I didn't stay up baking 'til midnight for nothing."

My father surrendered, and let his mother take over. Molly took out a piece of poster board, and started making a list of goods and prices.

"I figure we can make anywhere between $130 and $140 if we sell everything and get a couple of nice tips," Wil quickly figured.

"That brain of yours is always working," my grandma said as Wil grinned proudly.

Besides the fact that they were both incredibly intelligent people, Wil and my grandmother had one other thing in common. It had to do with dealing with the loss of a loved one. Wil's mother died from leukemia when Wil was in fifth grade. After Mrs. Thomas' death, my grandmother spent some time alone with Wil. I never felt right asking my grandmother what she said because I knew I would never truly understand. At the park, when the Ballplayers and I said we were sorry or asked Wil if she was OK, she changed the subject. The only thing I remember was something that happened in school. After some kids started teasing Wil for being so smart, she ran into the bathroom. I followed her in. She mumbled something about making a promise to her mother. I asked her to talk about it, but she just shook her head. After a while, we left it up to Wil to bring it up. I always said a prayer for Wil and her family every night before I went to sleep.

I looked around the party and saw more cars pulling into the lot and parking along the sides of the streets. Dozens of people popped open their trunks and unloaded coolers and lawn chairs. The music started booming, and the smell of charcoal starter grew thick in the air.

"This is gonna be a party!" Wil exclaimed. Then she took a bite of a chocolate cupcake.

"Come on, Wil," I said. "We've got to sell those."

"Sorry," she mumbled. "You know how I can't resist Mrs. O'Malley's cupcakes."

Whenever Wil started to get nervous about something, she did one of two things: she talked incessantly or ate whatever was in sight. And as the jump rope competition grew nearer, Wil had a hard time keeping her eyes off the table of sweets.

"We're taking turns running the table," I said. "Wil and Angel – you're first. We'll come back later."

"No more, Wil," Molly commanded before we left.

"All right, all right," Wil grumbled.

I looked to Angel and whispered, "Keep an eye on her."

Angel smiled. "Relax, P," she said. "I've got it covered."

Molly, Rosie and I walked around the park. We stopped on the field and kicked Molly's soccer ball around.

"How many days are we going to be at camp?" Rosie asked.

"'Til Saturday," Molly replied.

"Saturday?" Rosie gasped.

"Yeah," she replied. "What's wrong with Saturday?"

Rosie's eyes dropped down to the soccer ball. "I just didn't think it would be that long."

Rosalinda Jones was going into the sixth grade, which made her the youngest of our group. While she was as tough as her wiry frame, she hardly said a word unless it was really important. I began to wonder why she was so worried about camp. She couldn't be afraid of being homesick. It was only for a few days, and she'd be with us.

"You still want to go?" I asked.

"Yeah," she shot back. "I want to go."

Her eyes shifted away from me. I began to put it all together. With Rosie's brother Rico trying out for the big leagues, it was just Rosie and her parents at home. Mr. Jones had a reputation for pushing his kids harder than the rest of the parents, especially since Rosie was the only girl on the boys' all-star baseball team. She played well, but even I saw the pressure that she carried with her to every practice and every game. I thought taking a break from baseball would do her some good. But something else was going through Rosie's mind right then.

After rotating shifts four times, our sweets table was just about empty. J.J. walked up and bought our last cookie.

"What are you raising money for?" he asked.

"We're going to soccer camp," Molly answered.

"For real?" he asked.

"Yep," Molly said.

"That's not fair," J.J. said. "How come you get to go and we can't?"

"You got to go to basketball camp," Angel said. "Now it's our turn."

J.J. huffed. "Well, I'm glad to help out for such a good cause," he said as he dropped his change on the table. "Your going to soccer camp gets you out of my hair for a week."

"We're really going to miss you, J," Molly added with a smug grin.

J.J. smiled. "You're jumpin' today, right?" he asked.

"Yeah," I replied.

"I heard there are a lot of teams," J.J. added.

"Really?" Molly responded curiously.

J.J. was beginning to reel her in. "Yeah," he said. "And you'd better look out for the Kangaroos." He drew closer to us and lowered his voice into a raspy whisper. "They're the best squad. And of course, my cousin, Tasha, is on that team. Which means, you don't have a chance."

He threw his head back and burst into obnoxious laughter. All of us shook our heads.

"We've got it covered," I said confidently as J.J. strutted away.

"What's the total?" Wil asked Angel, who had been busy counting the dollars, while Rosie counted the coins.

"I've got $132," Angel said. She wrapped a rubber band around the wad of money and placed it in our aluminum lunch box.

"And I've got $4.50," Rosie added.

"That's a grand total of $136.50," Wil said proudly. "Just like I figured."

"And that's not including what you ate," I said with a smile.

"I didn't eat that much," Wil said. I tipped my head down and gave her one hard look. "OK, maybe a little more after you left," she admitted.

My grandmother walked over to the table as Angel neatly placed our money in the silver lunch box. "We've got so much more to save," Angel added resignedly.

"You gotta start somewhere," my grandma said. "Lemme lock up that box in the car before someone with sticky fingers comes along and helps themselves to it."

As my grandmother secured the box, I glanced at my watch. "We better start warming up."

I grabbed our rope and we weaved through the crowd. Some folks swayed to the music and laughed aloud. Others sat back and relaxed in lawn chairs, smiling with a plate of warm, tasty food in their hands. We all waved to our neighbors, relatives, and friends as we passed them by.

"Go get 'em girls!" Mrs. O'Malley cheered.

"Show 'em what you're made of Penny!" one of my uncles yelled.

I smiled and waved at all the people who cheered. Then I stopped right behind Wil.

"Wow," she said in amazement.

We stood at the edge of the basketball court, and watched as the fancy colored ropes swiveled in a smooth egg-beating motion. Some girls were jumping with a rope inside a rope. Another girl was leaping up and forming a split in the air.

"Look at her!" Angel said.

We all turned and saw a girl flip in the air, land on her feet and keep jumping.

"One, two, three..." Molly began counting softly, and her voice faded. "There are 15 teams!"

"Just a few more teams we have to beat," I said. "It doesn't matter."

Whether I believed what I was saying or not didn't matter. At least one of us had to remember how much time we prepared for this day. I wasn't about to throw in the towel before we even began.

"Wow," Angel echoed Wil's thoughts again.

"We can do it," I insisted.

When I smiled, Angel and Wil both looked at me and rolled their eyes. I felt my temperature rise ever so slightly.

"Don't go giving up now," I said forcing a smile to hide my frustration. "We're all in this together, and I'm not about to lose."

None of the Ballplayers ever thought that I got nervous or even upset about anything. They never saw me yell or shout in anger. No matter how much pressure fell on my shoulders, I took it upon myself to keep it together. After all, somebody had to. I turned my attention back to our competition and quickly observed that all the jumpers on each team had the same outfits.

"We don't look like a team if we're dressed in different clothes," I said. "We need to match."

"What are we gonna wear, P?" Molly said.

"How 'bout the Ballplayer uniforms?" I said.

"And if you'll let everyone use some of your headbands and wristbands," Angel said, "that will look cool."

"Yeah," I said. "My dad still has the uniforms in the front closet."

My father walked passed us. "Dad," I called out. He turned and looked down at us.

"What's up?" he asked.

"We're going to wear our Ballplayer uniforms for the jump rope contest."

"That's a good idea," he said. "Where are they?"

"At home," I said.

He smiled at us and said, "Which one of you is going to get them?"

"Since we're not old enough to drive, we're looking for a volunteer," I explained. I smiled as I asked, "Do I have any adult volunteers?"

My dad looked at me and grinned. He knew he owed me one for helping him with the lawn that morning. He left right away, and returned just in time for us to change and enter our team name into the competition. We had no other choice but to be called by what was written on our blue basketball T-shirts: *The Broadway Ballplayers.*

"Those are my girls out there!" my grandma called out as we began to practice. I looked over and smiled. I had a chance to make her and the rest of my family proud. I wasn't going to let them down.

After we had warmed up for about 10 minutes, the whistle blew. We followed instructions to sit on one side of the court. The director began calling out names in the order we were to perform. Our name was called at the very end of the list.

"The first round will begin in two minutes," one official said. "All compulsory jumpers should be on the right side. When it's your turn, you can join your teammates on the left."

I took one last look at Molly and gave her a big smile. Wil reached out and slapped her five.

"You're gonna do it, " Wil said. "Just like yesterday."

Molly took a deep breath and looked at me with that competitive fire in her blue eyes. She nodded, and then walked slowly over to join the rest of the jumpers.

Each player jumped for one minute at a time, and had two tries. The judges gave scores based on a 100-point scale and took off points for any type of error. Then they averaged the two scores together for a final score for each round.

I was glad we didn't go first. Two of the first six girls were so nervous that they messed up within 30 seconds. The highest score halfway through was a 78.

"Molly can beat that," I whispered to Wil, and she nodded.

The director announced, "Team 14 — The Kangaroos."

I looked up and saw J.J.'s cousin, Tasha, stretching out her legs.

"Uh-oh," Wil said quietly. We both looked right to Molly, who glared at Tasha. The two of them had clashed before in summer basketball league. Wil and I both knew that Molly's spat with Tasha was still fresh in her mind.

"Ready your ropes," the director said. The two twirlers bent down to the ground, grabbed hold of their ropes, and stood up.

When the horn blared, the twirlers stood up, and began swiveling the ropes at a comfortable speed. Tasha entered smoothly. She nailed her pop-ups, her kick-the-buckets, and the all-around as if she wrote the double-Dutch manual herself.

"Time!" the judge announced. The crowd erupted in whistles, hoots and cheers.

"That's my cuz!" J.J. shouted proudly.

"That was *tough!*" Wil said in awe. "I don't know how she can get any better than that."

Tasha scored a 91. When the judge held the score up, a hush fell over the crowd. Then more cheers followed. Molly looked over at me in a panic. I watched carefully as Tasha tipped her head arrogantly around at the crowd.

I leaned over and whispered to Wil, "She's gonna choke."

"Molly?" Wil shot back.

"No, Tasha," I said. "She's getting too cocky. She's gonna do something she can't do to beat her last score. Watch."

Tasha entered the ropes. Just as she got going, she called out for her teammates to twirl faster. And then even faster. But the twirlers couldn't stay together. All three of them were out of synch. Tasha got tangled in the ropes twice.

When the judge flashed a score of 70, I breathed a sign of relief. It left the Kangaroos with a disappointing first round score of 80.5. Tasha scowled at everyone and then plopped down on the ground. Molly anxiously jumped up from her spot.

"Team 15 — The Broadway Ballplayers," the director announced.

Our family and friends applauded as Wil and I neatly set our long rope on the ground.

"Go get 'em, Molly!" my dad cheered.

Tasha looked at Molly and scoffed. Then she turned to me.

"Hey, Penny!" she called out. "You're jumping with her? Why? You feel bad for her?" She threw her head back and laughed. "Good luck, Red," Tasha continued. "Try and stay on your feet for this game."

Calling Molly "Red" had nothing to do with her hair this time. Her face was beet red, a fiery red, an embarrassed and angry red. I turned to Tasha, who was still holding onto her smug grin, and smiled myself. Little did Tasha know that she was doing us a favor. She had made Molly mad, really mad. And when Molly got mad, she forgot all about how nervous she was.

"Don't look at her anymore," were my only words of advice to my best friend. She had to stay focused. "If you keep looking at her, we're gonna lose. Come on, Molly. Concentrate."

Molly took her place next to me, and then exhaled one deep breath. She smoothly entered the ropes, kept her position, and hit her first three sets of jumps perfectly. My nerves tingled as the crowd roared. *Hang in there!* Twenty seconds left. *You're almost there.* Ten seconds left and she was still looking smooth. *You got it.* Five, four, three, two...

The whistle shrieked. I dropped my rope and gave Molly a hard high five, and then Wil did the same.

"Yeah, yeah!" I said when a score of 85 went up on the board. Molly grinned proudly, and then she took a deep breath. We all knew it was far from over.

"Now just do the same exact thing," I told Molly for the second jump. "Nothing fancy."

She nodded as she fixed her glare on the rope.

"Ready your ropes," the judge called out.

The horn blared. Molly looked comfortable until she looked down. When she noticed her shoelace, her eyes grew wide. My heart fluttered, but I knew I couldn't look scared. If I did, Molly would sense it right away, lose her concentration, and we wouldn't have a chance.

"Don't worry about it," I whispered as I kept a straight face. "Just keep jumping."

With about 20 seconds left, Molly tripped, and the crowd gasped. With hesitation, she quickly got out of the ropes and re-entered. Once she stepped back inside the ropes, she did not falter again.

Our weakest link had become our biggest strength. At the end of round one, we were in first place.

But it was far from over.

Chapter Five

As the heavy heat poured down onto our tired bodies, our patience began to crumble. It seemed like we were never going to get through round two, especially after the judges mixed up two scores, and then disqualified one team for being too late for their turn.

"What's taking so long?" a man yelled from the crowd during a break. "Let's get this over with."

Wil sat cross-legged on the grass as she waited in line by herself. I watched her carefully as she leaned forward and began scratching a rock onto the blacktop. Every few seconds, she closed her eyes beneath her glasses and took a deep breath.

"She doesn't look good," Molly said to me.

"Maybe it's the heat," I said. "She'll be all right."

"She needs somebody to talk to," Molly said. "You know how much she talks when she gets nervous."

I looked at Wil, and hoped that she would hang in there. *Just a few more minutes, and we'll be right there with you.*

Our turn finally came. I looked at the scoreboard and it was the same situation as in the first round. We had to beat the Kangaroos, who finished the speed round with an impressive 85 points.

As we laid our ropes on the ground, I said softly, "Let's do it!"

Then I looked up and my eyes grew wide. Sweat trickled down Wil's pale face as she rubbed her stomach.

"What's wrong?" I asked.

"Nothing," she replied.

"You sure?" I asked again.

"My stomach hurts a little," she said. "That's all."

I had a funny feeling that it wasn't her nerves and it wasn't the heat.

"You ate too many cupcakes at the bake sale, didn't you?" I asked.

She winced pathetically, hoping for some sympathy.

"Oh grcat," Molly rolled her eyes as she took a deep breath. "Just great. And you were worried about me."

"I'll bet that you ate just as much as me," Wil shot back.

"I only had three," Molly said.

"We'll be all right," I said to calm everyone down. "Just don't think about it."

I picked through the crowd and finally spotted Angel. She looked at me and shrugged her shoulders. I took a deep breath and turned back to my partner.

"Are you gonna be all right?" I asked. "Or should I get Angel to jump for you?"

"No," Wil said as she straightened up. "I'll be all right."

"Oh, great," Molly groaned. "I can't believe this!"

One judge called out, "Ready your ropes, girls."

"You can do it Wil," I whispered. "Take one minute at a time."

We started the ropes, and Wil jumped in. She moaned as her feet tapped on the pavement. She spent the entire minute stuck in first gear. There was no speed, no spunk. Nothing. The whistle blew and she was done. When the judge flashed a low score of 80, I saw the Kangaroos grin confidently.

"Forget that one," I said. "You've got another chance."

But Wil's second jump was no better.

"Sorry," she said dejectedly after she was finished. "I think I'd better sit down."

There was a long silence as we all stared at the scoreboard. We needed a miracle. Molly turned to me and said, "You can do it, Penny. You won't screw up. You never screw up."

"Yeah," Wil added. "If anybody can pull us out of this mess – it's you."

I was being asked to do the impossible. Just before I tried to explain this, I took one look at Molly's sunburned face and weary eyes. All her practice and determination had paid off for her. Then I watched as Wil took off her glasses and rubbed her brow. If we lost, all the kids from Broadway would let her hear about it, and she'd blame herself for everything. My friends were counting on me. I had to believe that I could do it.

"There's a special announcement," a judge called out. "Because of the heat, we're allowing each jumper only one try in the freelance competition."

All eyes fell on me. I grinned, thinking of the one-shot deal. Wil reached out and patted me on the back. "It's all you, P," she said.

A man from the crowd called out, "Put on a show, Sweet P. Show 'em what you got."

I kept right on smiling as if this was the way I had planned it all along. I sat by myself watching the last round. Each jumper seemed to get better and better. When I saw all their fancy moves and flips, I decided that my routine of simple steps wouldn't be good enough. I needed something extraordinary.

"Sammy!" I called out. Within seconds, my little brother came running. "Could you please get my ball?" I asked.

He nodded and sprinted away. I turned my attention back to the jumpers. When the Kangaroos scored 92 points, my eyes wandered over to my grandmother, who was sitting right across from me. She nodded her head, clenched her fist, and smiled. I then turned to my father. He grinned proudly. Everyone wanted me to be in this situation.

I glanced up to the scoreboard to compare our score with the Kangaroos. It read:

	Round #1 Compulsory	Round #2 Speed	Round #3 Freelance
#14 Kangaroos	80.5	85	92
#15 Ballplayers	81.5	80	

"Molly, you gotta stall for me," I whispered.

She scrunched up her nose and asked, "Why?"

"I just need two minutes," I explained.

Molly started jumping up and down. She winced as she turned to the judges and asked, "May I please use the bathroom?"

"All right," the official said. "Hurry. We'll figure out what your partner needs to win."

"What do I need, Wil?" I asked.

"At least a 96 to tie," she replied.

"You mean a 97 to win," I said.

Wil nodded her head and smiled. "You can get it. I know you can."

I wondered how many people at the park would have wanted to be in my shoes at that moment. Then I wondered how many people I would disappoint if I didn't pull through. I took a deep breath. Then I felt a tug on my shirt. I looked down, and saw Sammy holding my basketball.

"Here," he said, and he handed me the ball.

"Thanks," I said.

"Are you gonna win, Penny?" he asked. His face was serious, and I could tell he was thinking hard about something. "Everybody says you're gonna win."

Even Sammy knew that was not a reasonable question for anyone. But for some reason, he thought I could explain it all, and tell him what was going to happen. I looked in his big wide eyes and saw that he was counting on me, too.

"I'm going to try my best," I said.

I patted him on the head. Then Wil and I walked to center court. "What are you gonna do, P?" Wil asked.

I bounced the ball on the ground three times and said, "Just wait. You'll see."

When Molly returned from the outhouse and saw the basketball tucked under my arm, her eyes sparkled. The crowd began to cheer.

"Sweet P is up!" a kid called out. "Look out!"

"Let's go, Penny!" Mr. O'Malley cheered. "You got it, kid!"

Keep it fun. Keep it fun. No pressure. No pressure.

"Ready your ropes," the judge said for the last time that day. "Begin!"

I ran into the ropes with the ball on my hip. I started passing the ball around my waist, and then around my head. I slapped it hard, hoping the noise would create a beat with my hands, the ropes and my feet. It worked. The crowd started clapping to my beat, and I knew it was time to add to my repertoire. I bounced the ball down with my right hand, and then my left. Then I bent down and bounced it twice quickly.

"Go Ballplayers...Go Ballplayers!" I heard J.J. yell.

"Uh-huh, uh-huh," a woman shouted. "Look at her go!"

I spun around dribbling. With about 10 seconds to go, I started bouncing the ball between my legs.

"You gotta dribble out," Molly whispered anxiously. "We need the extra points."

I burst out through the ropes as if they were on fire. When I landed safely, the whistle blew, and the crowd roared triumphantly.

"Yes!" Wil yelled. Both Molly and Wil ran up and hugged me.

"That's my girl!" my grandmother yelled.

"Way to go, Penny!" my mother shouted.

My father was smiling as if he had just done it all himself. Rosie and Angel jumped from the crowd and joined us as we waited for the score.

"I've never seen you do that," Rosie said in awe. "That was great!"

"You were incredible!" Angel said.

"Yo, Penny!" J.J. called out over the celebration. "We're not calling you Sweet P anymore. We're calling you Sweet Feet. I'll take a pair of whatever you're wearing!"

When the judge held up the scorecard, Molly screeched like a wild animal. My score of 98 was two points shy of perfection, but good enough for the victory.

"You did it!" Molly screamed. "I can't believe it...I just can't believe it," she kept repeating softly to herself with the palm of her hand stuck on her forehead. "I don't know how..."

The judge handed us an envelope and three bright green T-shirts that read:

DOUBLE DUTCH
CHAMPS

Chapter Six

The jump roping contest was over, but the party wasn't.

"Penny," J.J. called out. "You wanna play?"

I nodded my head as I pulled the wristbands up on my forearm.

"Full court?" Wil gasped.

J.J. nodded.

"I don't know, P," Wil moaned.

"We're in," I told J.J.

I raced to the water fountain for a quick drink. By the time I made it to the courts, they were already arguing.

"I wanna be captain," Eddie said.

"You're always captain," Wil shot back.

"Let's shoot for teams," I offered.

"No," J.J. said. "That always takes too long. Let Penny and Mike be captains."

Nobody objected. I looked at Mike and gave him first pick. He picked Eddie. I picked Molly. He chose J.J. Then I looked around carefully searching the crowd to make the best possible selection for my team. My eyes stopped at Billy Flanigan. His eyes shifted nervously to the ground, and his face turned red. He had been through this so many times before. The fear of being picked last. The humiliation of not being chosen at all.

"I'll take Billy," I said.

Billy's worried face broke into a sheepish grin. As he jogged over and stood next to me, Mike snickered. He couldn't believe that I had picked Billy Flanigan.

"Hah!" J.J. scoffed and then he smiled at Mike. They were both banking on an easy win.

"Would you pick, Mike?" Molly called out impatiently. "Come on!"

Mike stopped smiling and said, "I got Rosie."

I turned to Wil, who was clutching her T-shirt over her stomach. I felt bad for forcing her into this. Maybe she was really sick this time. "Are you sure you're all right to play, Wil?" I asked.

"Yeah," she groaned and winced in pain. "I'm all right," she added.

"I got Wil then," I said. Then I saw Cowboy stroll up to the courts.

"Yo!" he called out. "Can I get in?"

Mike was down to his last pick. He bit his lip and held his chin. I knew he wanted to use it on Cowboy. But he hesitated for one reason that had nothing to do with basketball. Dennis "Cowboy" Thorpe was kind of my boyfriend or that's what everybody else called him.

"Who's got the next pick?" Cowboy asked.

I looked at Mike. "Go ahead," I told him.

I didn't care. I just wanted to play, and I certainly was not going to change my mind and trade Wil for Cowboy. So Mike picked him. Cowboy smiled bashfully at me as I passed, and then muttered, "We're gonna kick your butt." I looked at him and laughed.

"You got the last pick, Penny," Molly reminded me.

I took a quick look around. Angel took off, so it was between Sleepy and Marvin. Sleepy was popular, friendly and a decent ballplayer. I wish I could have said the same about Marvin. I wouldn't call Marvin a bad kid. He just had a sly way of doing things. Although he never really talked much, the bags under his eyes and his worn, dirty clothes said it all. With an alcoholic mother and a father who was in and out of jail, it was up to Marvin to raise his little sister, Maddy, practically all by himself. They didn't have much money, and when they needed it, Marvin found a way to get it by any means possible. This was no secret to any of us. When something was missing in the neighborhood, everybody pointed the finger at Marvin.

I felt bad for the kid, and then I felt bad for feeling sorry for him. I was torn between trying to justify why he did what he did, and knowing that what he did wasn't right.

"Any day now, Penny," Eddie groaned.

"I got Marvin," I said.

Everyone hustled into position and the game started. Within five minutes, bodies pushed and shoved each other around.

"Come on, Eddie!" J.J. screamed. "Play some D, man."

"I got Mike," I yelled. "Molly, you take J."

Molly hacked J.J., but he didn't call the foul. J.J. slapped me on the next play, and I let it go, too. For a moment, I thought we were going to remain civil with one another. But I was wrong. Within two minutes, everyone was fouling, whining, and calling each other names. Eddie drove to the basket, and leaped in the air. Marvin jumped over to block his shot and smacked him in midair. Eddie went crashing down to the ground.

"Whad'ya do that for?" Eddie screamed.

Marvin cowered as he shrugged. Eddie's eyes were like daggers driving into Marvin's thin body. When I slid in between the two of them, Eddie tried to push me out of the way. I grabbed his arm and did not move.

"Let it go, Eddie," I said. "He didn't mean it. Everybody's fouling. Don't take everything so personally."

"Why are you always standing up for him?" Eddie shot back. "He's a thief!"

Before I could even think about what to say next, Marvin screamed, jumped forward and pushed me into Eddie. I stumbled, and then regained my balance as Cowboy, Molly, and J.J. came to the rescue.

"Relax, Marvin!" I screamed. "He didn't mean it!"

Molly and Cowboy grabbed Marvin around the chest, and J.J. threw his arms around Eddie.

"Why don't you grow up, Eddie?" yelled Molly, who was always the first to hurl a rotten insult at Eddie. "You're a loser."

That wasn't exactly what anyone wanted to hear. But it was enough to take the pressure off Marvin. Eddie turned to Molly, and they started shouting back and forth.

"Mind your own business," Eddie yelled. "Can't you keep your big mouth shut?"

"Cut it out, and just play," I said firmly.

Everyone else had returned to their positions, and J.J. checked the ball in quickly. Within minutes the heat became too much to bear. The only thing that pulled our bodies up and down the floor was the score. Our game was tied at 13 each.

"Win by two," J.J. called out.

On the next possession, I snuck up behind Cowboy while he was dribbling and picked his pocket clean. I scooped up the ball and dribbled down to the other end and scored. Three teenagers, who were hanging out under the basket laughed at Cowboy, and then started razzing him.

"You can't touch her, man," one kid called out. "She's the real deal. Just like her old man."

Cowboy didn't say anything as I hustled back on defense. J.J. missed a shot and Marvin grabbed the rebound. I gave it to Billy and he dribbled right into the corner, and picked up the ball. Billy did this every time he got the ball, and it really ticked his teammates off. Two players always converged on him, and he threw the ball up frantically. Luckily this time, it bounced off J.J.'s hand and it was still our ball.

"Don't keep doing that!" Wil yelled at Billy in frustration. "It doesn't work."

"No, keep doing it," Eddie joked. "Keep dribbling into the corner and getting stuck."

When I heard Eddie's sarcastic tone, my blood boiled. My father had taught Billy in his special education class, and said what a kind, gentle person Billy was. I looked at Eddie as he grinned and shook

53

my head in disgust. "You got it, Billy," I said calmly. "If you're open just shoot it. You're money from that corner spot."

He nodded his head nervously. Molly passed him the ball on the next possession. He looked up to the basket. His eyes shifted to the corner spot, but he did not move. I yelled his name as I slashed to the basket. He bounce-passed me the ball right as two people went to cover him. I hit the running lay-up, and we won the game.

"Yeah, Bill," I said as I gave him high five. His eyes lit up as he slapped my hand firmly.

Cowboy reached out his hand, and I slapped him five.

"Good game," he said. "I saw you jumping to-day. You were pretty good. But you're lucky that I wasn't jumping."

I laughed at Cowboy. He always talked big. He earned his nickname one Halloween when he dressed up as a cowboy. He wore his cowboy boots all the time, and pretended that he had a drawl. I liked Cowboy because he was funny without being mean to others. He was kind of cute, too. I wasn't sure if we were boyfriend and girlfriend, seeing each other or going together. Whatever you want to call it, it wasn't anything big. He called me on the phone one night, and I called him back two nights later. Ever since, all the kids on Broadway Ave. and at the park just kind of assumed we were together. Whatever that meant.

"Are you gonna be at the park tomorrow?" he asked.

"Yeah," I said. "Probably."

"Maybe I'll ride over," he said as we walked to the water fountain. I didn't walk or stand too close to him. I always feared that he would try and hold my hand around my friends or near the courts. Fortunately, he never did.

"Penny," J.J. called out as he came running over to me. "This high school kid over here thinks he can beat you. I've been telling him he's crazy. Come over and kick his butt."

I shook my head, knowing the only reason why this kid wanted to play me was because I was a girl.

"It's not a girl-boy thing," J.J. assured me. "It's because you're good."

J.J. knew that I didn't like being put on a stage even though it happened to me all the time. In school, at the park, and anywhere I went in the city, some poor sucker with an ego would think he could beat me.

"Just one game to five?" J.J. begged.

"How much money do you have on it?" I asked.

"Ten bucks," J.J. replied.

J.J. always bet with money he didn't have. I just shook my head as I looked into the distance, and saw this sorry looking guy with gold chains around his neck trying to play ball. His feet were heavy, his arms were too strong and bulky. He could barely make a lay-up.

"This will be quick," I said as I walked toward the court.

"It's on!" J.J. called out.

I didn't even know this kid's name, and I didn't want to find out. I walked through the motions and missed easy shots on purpose. At the end of the game, he laughed and smiled, thinking he was really cool. He went over to J.J., and said, "Pay up."

J.J. looked at me and his mouth dropped open. He was lost for words. He was so hurt, so destroyed by the disappointment of my losing that I thought he was going to cry.

"Double or nothing," I called out.

J.J.'s eyes lit up, and he flashed his loopy smile.

The boy turned to me, and said, "Fine. Let's go."

He even felt so bad for me that he gave me the ball first. Big mistake. All it took were five shots. I sunk every one of them. He didn't even get a chance to touch the ball. After the first three baskets, his friends were laughing hysterically at him. J.J. asked them if they wanted to play me next, and they quickly said no.

When it was over, J.J. strutted up and proudly collected the money he had wagered on me. Then he turned and walked toward me.

"Here's your half," he said as he handed me the money.

"I don't want it," I muttered.

"Just take it," he said. "Give it away like you usually do. That chump deserves to go home with empty pockets."

J.J. and I had been through this before. In games that meant nothing to me, I usually told the kid I beat to keep his money. After taking away his pride, I had to leave him with something.

"You'd better take it, Penny," J.J. said. "You earned it."

I took the money and stuck it in my sock. "It will be for soccer camp," I said.

"Good," J.J. replied. "It's nice to see you've finally come to your senses."

Molly, Angel, Wil, and Rosie had been shooting down at the other end while I was playing. I walked down to shoot with them just as Mr. Gordon walked onto the court.

"Hey, Mr. G," Wil called out. "We made $136.50 at the bake sale."

"That's good," he said.

"And we won the jump rope competition," Angel added. "So that's an extra 50 bucks. You should have seen Penny do all this crazy stuff with the basketball. And Molly did great too."

"I heard all about it," he assured us. "I'm really proud of you girls."

"How are we gonna make more money?" Rosie asked.

"That's up to you to decide," Mr. Gordon replied. "What do you think?"

"I hadn't thought about that yet," Molly said.

"How about a car wash?" I asked.

"Yeah," Rosie said.

"That will be fun," Molly added. "Maybe down at the park."

"But where will we get a hose?" asked Wil, who was always thinking one step ahead of us. "There's no hose at the park."

"What about at Lincoln?" I asked.

"I'll see if I can hook something up for you."

"All right!" Wil said. "We'll be there tomorrow at two."

"I'll be a little late," Angel said. "I don't get back from my church until after two."

"Just meet us after you get back," I told Angel.

"I'll see you tomorrow," Mr. Gordon added as he walked off. "Have fun at the rest of the party and..."

"Be safe," Wil interrupted. "We know, Mr. G."

He looked back over his shoulder and smiled.

Chapter Seven

A ngel wasn't the only one of us who had to attend church service on Sunday. My grandmother began hustling us out of the house at 8:15 a.m.

"We're gonna be late," she called out. "Let's go!"

Of course we arrived 20 minutes early, which made us one of the first families to walk up the church steps. As the congregation filtered through the doors, I slowly began to forget about how tired I felt. Dozens of smiling people greeted family, friends, and strangers with the same amount of warmth and friendliness. My mother and father started catching up with people in the neighborhood, and Sammy ran off with one of his friends. Just as I turned to look for my cousin, I spotted Reverend James.

"Good morning young lady," he called out. "You put on quite a show at the jump rope contest yesterday. How'd you do it?"

I smiled and said, "I kept the faith."

It was not only the perfect answer for me to tell a preacher — it was the truth. He grinned and gave me a hug.

"Reverend James," I asked. "Will you make an announcement about a car wash we're having today at Lincoln? We're trying to raise money to go to soccer camp."

"I sure will," he said just as the organist started playing.

When Sammy ran by me, I whispered, "Go sit with Mom and Dad." He skipped down the aisle and took his seat. Then he turned to watch as I took my place in line with the rest of the children's choir at the back of the church. I swayed down the aisle with my friends as we sang. When the beat of our hands clapping and the ringing of our voices came to an end, Reverend James gave his invocation, and allowed others to share their words. After another song, Reverend James walked up to the podium to deliver his sermon. I wasn't one who always paid close attention to speakers, but when Reverend James spoke, I listened. He quoted Booker T. Washington that day and explained the quote so many times, and in so many different ways that it eventually stuck in my head.

"Character, not circumstance, makes the person," he repeated.

"Amen!" a woman called out.

Reverend James turned to us and called out, "I want all of you children to understand what it means to have character, and that you must maintain that character regardless of the circumstance."

His eyes locked into mine, and I nodded my head. After his closing comments, we stood on our feet and belted out another hymn. When it came time for special announcements, Reverend James stepped up to the microphone.

"Penny asked me to tell all of you that the kids on Broadway are having a car wash today at Lincoln School," he said as he turned to me and grinned. "I'm trusting that Penny will make sure to throw on a little extra car wax for all the people of the congregation."

Everyone laughed, and I smiled. After Reverend James gave his benediction, we swayed down the aisle as we sang our final song.

• • • •

Later that afternoon, Mr. O'Malley cruised down Broadway Avenue in his beat up old station wagon and stopped at the corner of Woodside and Broadway. Rosie and I piled into the car.

"Angel's not back from church yet?" Wil asked.

"No," I said. "She'll be getting out of church in about a half-hour."

"Is your dad coming?" Molly asked.

"Yeah," I said. "He had to run some errands. He said he'd catch up with us."

Molly's little sister, Annie, crawled onto my lap.

"Penny," she asked. "Can I wear your headband?"

Annie's tiny hands gently pulled the headband off my head. Then she stretched it over her head of shaggy, thin hair and twisted it around enough so that her ears stuck out on the sides.

"Let me fix it for you," I offered.

She dropped her hands down. I straightened her out and said, "There you go."

"Do I look like Penny?" Annie asked and she looked around to everyone.

Nobody answered.

"I wanna be cool just like you," Annie said as she turned to me. "I want to score all the points and be the best!"

My friends continued staring out the windows.

"I think you should just be Annie," I said quietly. "Just be yourself."

I gazed out the window. I thought about my mother telling me not to fret over things I couldn't control. But being only 12 years old, it was tough not to worry about what others thought of me. I wondered if I would ever be able to play without anyone knowing who I was, and without one person wishing to be like me.

When we pulled into the empty parking lot of Lincoln Grade School, I spotted Mr. Gordon next to the building. He looked up as he fidgeted with the nozzle of the hose.

"Good afternoon girls," he said. "Everybody ready to do some work today?"

"I've got the signs, Mr. G," Molly said. "Where should I put 'em up?"

"One on the telephone pole, and one on that fence over there," he said as he pointed.

Mr. O'Malley set down the buckets of soap and brushes. "I'll help you," he offered.

"Now if we're not getting too many cars here, maybe we can head closer to the park," Mr. Gordon said. "A lot more folks know you girls there and I'm sure they'll be willing to pitch in."

"Where can we use a hose?" Wil asked.

"At your building," Mr. Gordon replied. "I talked to the landlord at the party yesterday. He said we could use the water for an hour or two."

Mr. O'Malley set us up into stations. Rosie and I rinsed. Mr. O'Malley and his sons Frankie and Kevin scrubbed tires. Molly and Wil soaped and washed. We all took turns helping Mr. Gordon dry until Angel and my father joined us later.

Business was slow at the start. Our eyes followed the oncoming cars with a look of hope that faded into another deep breath as they passed us by.

Only five cars stopped in the first hour.

"Maybe we should just stop people at the light and tell them how filthy their cars are," Wil suggested.

"Yeah," Molly said. She went back to the trunk and drew up one more sign. She held it up with a proud smile. It read: **Your car needs a bath.**

"What do ya think?" she asked.

"It's corny," I said, "but then again, so are you."

Molly turned to her brother Frankie. "If you stand on the corner and hold this sign over your head, I'll buy you something at the store later," she offered. Frankie's face perked up. He scampered out to the road, running with the cardboard sign over his shoulder like a cape.

Sure enough, within 10 minutes we had five cars waiting. Most of the people who pulled in were folks from church. I gave a little extra effort on their cars, knowing I had to hold true to the promise I had made to Reverend James.

"Let's move it," Wil shouted. "Move it, move it, move it!"

We scrubbed and rinsed for over an hour and a half.

"How many have we done?" I called out to Wil.

"This will be number 20," she said. She looked up thoughtfully into the sky. "We washed eight blue cars, five black, three red, two green, and two white."

I shook my head at her in amazement.

"You're the only person on this planet who would remember such a thing," Molly said.

"What?" she said defensively. "I gotta keep my mind doing somethin'."

At four o'clock, Mr. Gordon decided to make the move over to Broadway to cash in before dusk. We set up in front of the Uptown Apartments. With the music beating down from a second floor apartment, we danced around for a few minutes. Then it was straight back to work.

"Hey," I heard a voice call. I turned and it was Cowboy and his friend Beef Potato. Beef's real name was either Ronald or Donald, but we called him Beef like everyone else. Rumor was that his brother nicknamed him Beef for his hearty appetite, and then somebody else gave him the last name of Potato.

"Do you wash bikes, too?" Beef asked.

"If you've got five bucks," Wil replied.

"I don't think my bike is even worth five bucks," Cowboy joked.

"What do you guys have planned this afternoon?" my dad asked.

"Nothin'," Beef said and he shrugged.

"Then grab a towel," Mr. Gordon said. "Cowboy, you dry, and Beef, you can rinse."

The boys huffed, dropped their bikes, grumbled some words between themselves, and then walked over to join us.

"You kids have to stay busy," Mr. Gordon said. "Idle hands are the devil's workshop."

There it was again. I looked at Mr. G and shook my head.

Why not say something positive? Why not mention how we didn't get into trouble or how we stuck together and did as we were asked?

"Penny, you're in charge of making sure that either your father or Mr. O'Malley get every dollar that's in the lunch box. Don't let it out of your sight. Is that clear?"

I nodded. "I got it covered, Mr. G," I said.

Five minutes later, J.J., Eddie, Sleepy, Billy, Mike, and Marvin all had wandered over from the courts. Within seconds, my father had them soaping, rinsing, and drying.

"We're playing after we're through," J.J. said to me. "And we're taking all this extra work out on you. Count on it."

"Man, how much longer?" Eddie whined.

"Three more cars and we're done," Wil said.

"How much money have you made so far?" Marvin asked.

"Over $200," Molly said proudly.

Wil walked over to the silver lunch box and slid in three $10 bills. Just as she went to slam it shut, it slipped off the stoop and crashed to the ground. All eyes turned to the money on the ground. Wil frantically picked it up and slapped it in her hand.

"Sorry," she said. "I didn't mean it. Don't worry, I got it."

For a split second I thought about what we had all seen. Money. Easy money. And lots of it.

"Let's go play," J.J. shouted.

"We've got to finish picking up," Molly said. We hung all the towels over the ledge. Eddie picked one up and turned it into a whip. Soon everybody started running around and smacking each other with towel whips. I looked around again at all the kids running around, and then glanced at the silver lunch box. "Where's the money?" I asked calmly.

"The what?" Mike said.

"The money," I said. "It was right here."

Mr. O'Malley stood up from behind his station wagon.

"What's with the money?" he asked.

"My dad has it," I said coolly, and I smiled. "He must have taken it."

My heart skipped a beat. I wanted so badly for my father to have taken the money home. I wasn't sure, but Mr. O'Malley believed me.

"All right, then," he said and he turned to his children. "Molly, Annie and Frankie, you're in the house at eight. Not a second later."

As soon as Mr. O'Malley got in the car and started his engine, we all started blurting out questions.

"Where is it?"

"Does Mr. H have it?"

"Whoever took it better give it back."

"Don't say a word to any adults," I said. "Not until we get this straightened out."

My father pushed through the front doors. All eyes turned to him.

He grinned as he asked, "What are you kids up to now?"

"We're gonna play some soccer on the field to get ready for camp," I said.

"All right then," he said. "You and your brother are home by eight."

Then he looked at the empty aluminum box. "Where's the money?"

My eyes looked down at the ground.

"My dad has it," Molly said coolly.

I looked at her, breathed a sigh of relief, and then felt crummy all over again. When my father left, everyone gathered around in a tight huddle.

"Who took it?" Molly looked around and yelled at everyone. "Just admit it. Who took it?"

"This isn't right," Wil said. "That was our money. We worked hard for that money."

"Hold up!" I called out. "Yelling at each other isn't gonna do us any good."

"We all know who did it," J.J. said. "Look around. Guess who's not here."

I glanced around desperately wanting to see Marvin among us. But he was nowhere to be found.

"Not again," Angel mumbled.

What Marvin did made everyone angry and miserable. So many times we thought he had taken something, but we never had any evidence. Some kids got so fed up with it that they tried to set him up just so they could frame him. But they never caught Marvin.

"I told you he was a thief," Eddie yelled. "You got yourself a problem. We're out of this one. Let's go."

While a bunch of the boys followed Eddie down to the park, J.J. and Cowboy stayed behind. I started looking around the porch and in the bushes. "Maybe it got lost somewhere in here," I said.

"You know he took it," Cowboy said to me and he shook his head. "Somebody's got to talk to that kid."

"What are we gonna tell Mr. G?" Molly asked. "He's gonna be so mad."

"Somebody has to go get it back from Marvin," Wil said.

"Who's gonna do it?" Rosie asked.

"I'd do it," Cowboy said, "but I don't know him that well. It's got to be somebody from Broadway."

"I'll do it," Molly offered.

That was not a good idea. If Molly went to get it back, she'd probably smack poor Marvin upside the head. Then Marvin would deny it, and we'd never see the money again. I looked around at the rest of my friends. J.J. walked away. Cowboy shrugged as he followed right behind him. I turned to the rest of the Ballplayers. Wil would be too nervous to approach Marvin. Rosie was too shy. Angel could have done it, but she didn't know Marvin as well as the rest of us.

"I'll do it," I said. "As long as nobody says a word to him. If we jump all over his case, he'll deny it. Then we'll never get it back."

"You'd better talk to him before he spends it all," Wil said.

"It's late, and I've got to be in by eight," I said. "I don't have enough time tonight. And if I come in late, my father's going to want to know why, and then he'll be mad at me for not telling him what happened."

"Do it first thing in the morning," Angel added.

Everyone agreed that I had to get up first thing in the morning and take care of the situation. After kicking the soccer ball around on the field for a few minutes, we walked to the corner of Woodside and Broadway and called it a night.

"I hope you get it back," Wil said to me as she went inside her apartment building.

I said good-bye to Molly and Rosie, and they turned west down Broadway Ave. Angel and I walked east down Broadway together.

"Are you nervous?" Angel asked.

"About what?" I said.

"Talking to Marvin," she replied.

"Nah," I said. "I'll think about it tonight."

My friend was called Angel for a good reason. When Angela Russomano wasn't at the park playing ball or hanging out with us, she was at church with her family. I could always count on her for good advice.

"Marvin's a good kid," Angel said. "I believe it. But somebody has to talk to him and tell him that."

"He's gonna get mad at me," I muttered.

"You're doing him a favor," she called out as she walked up her porch. "You may be the only one who can help him."

Angel pulled open her front door and took a deep breath. "Good luck, P," she said. "I'll see you tomorrow."

As I walked along by myself, I tried to do as my grandmother always told me. In my mind, I climbed into Marvin's body and tried to see things through his eyes. After a few seconds, I realized I couldn't do it. I came from a strong family with a mom and dad and grandmother who loved me. I was athletic, smart, and popular. Everyone wanted to be my friend. I believed in hope and goodness. I laid

69

awake that night, staring through the darkness. I replayed what I would say to Marvin over and over in my mind. I thought of every kind of reaction he could give me and how I would handle it.

With all of my friends depending on me, I had no idea what the next day would bring.

Chapter Eight

When my alarm buzzed loudly at 7 a.m., I smacked the snooze button, and groaned. I wanted so badly to fall back asleep, but I couldn't. My mind raced with thoughts of dealing with Marvin. *I could ask him to give me half back. Or maybe I could give him $50 or $75 – just for food money.* Then I huffed in frustration. *If I had just told Mr. G the truth, he'd go and get it back from Marvin. Why was I putting myself through this?*

I pulled my body out of bed and walked into the kitchen. My grandmother sat reading the paper and sipping her coffee at the kitchen table. When I walked through the doorway, she raised her eyebrows in disbelief.

"Do you know what time it is?" she asked.

I nodded.

"What are you doing up so early?"

"I have to do something," I said.

"What?" she said.

"I have to talk to someone about camp."

"When are you leaving?" she asked.

"Wednesday," I said.

My grandmother walked across the kitchen and grabbed a small box off the desk.

"I picked up some stationary yesterday so you can write me while you're at camp," my grandmother told me.

I didn't understand why she insisted I had to write. She only lived on the other side of the city, and I would be back long before she received the mail.

"I'm only going to be gone for a few days," I muttered.

"I know," she said. "But I want you to write every day. Otherwise, you might forget all the fun things you did."

I wasn't paying too much attention to what she said after that. I just sat down at the table and ate my breakfast in silence. Then I felt the weight of my grandmother's stare.

"Are you going to tell me what you're up to this morning," she asked, "or am I going to have to follow you out of this house and chase you around all day?"

There was no getting out of this one. She was not kidding about chasing me around all day.

"As long as you don't tell my mom or dad," I said and I gave her a serious look. "Promise?"

She nodded and I went on with my story.

"Yesterday after the car wash, Mr. G. put me in charge of watching the money. We all started fooling around, and the next thing I knew, the money was gone. Then everybody started yelling at each other. We all know who has it."

"Who?"

"Marvin," I said. "He takes everything. The kid doesn't have anything."

"That doesn't make it right," she said firmly.

"Dad asked me where the money was yesterday," I added. "I told him that Mr. O'Malley had it." I paused knowing it was time to admit that what I did was wrong. "I know I shouldn't have lied."

"You got that right," she shot back. When she shook her head, my insides began to hurt.

"Please promise that you won't tell him," I pleaded. "I have to get it all straightened out before word gets back to Mr. G."

"And how are you going to do that?" she asked.

"I'm going to talk to Marvin this morning," I said and then my eyes dropped down to my cereal. "I don't know what he's going to do. I don't want him to get mad at me."

She raised her voice and said, "He has no right to get mad at you. You have the right to get what belongs to you and your friends."

"You think I should give him part of it?" I asked.

"No!" she shot back firmly. "Don't pity him. It will only make him think that what he did was acceptable. It's not!"

"Well, maybe Mr. G can send him to a camp," I said. "Maybe he's jealous."

My grandmother kept shaking her head. "What he did was wrong. You can't keep rewarding someone when they're doing wrong."

"I have to give him something," I said.

My grandmother stood up and walked over to the kitchen sink. She bent over, opened the cupboard and pulled out a brown bag. She went to the refrigerator and reached for a carton of milk and a dozen eggs. Then she went to the cupboard and grabbed a loaf of bread, three cans of soup, a box of pasta, and canned vegetables. She walked back to the table and set the bag in front of me.

"This is the only thing you should give him for now," she said. "He needs to find an honest way to earn everything else."

With my arms around the heavy brown bag, I dragged myself out the front door, and down Broadway Ave. Three blocks later, I started to slow down. When I came within a stone's throw of Marvin's house, my nerves began to tingle.

I walked up his stairs and rested the brown bag on my hip. I took one long look at the doorbell. In fear of waking up Marvin's mother, I rapped lightly on the wooden door. Nobody answered. I eyed the doorbell again. I pressed it. It didn't work. I couldn't take it anymore. I went back to the door, and pounded it solidly with my fist.

I heard a little girl call out, "Who's there?"

"It's Penny," I said after I recognized Maddy's voice. I hoped that she would remember me. "I'm Marvin's friend."

I thought for a second about what I had just said. I called myself a friend. *Did Marvin have any true friends? Would a friend do what I was doing?*

The door creaked open. A little girl with tangled hair, pale blue eyes and a dirty face peeped her head from behind the knob. She eyed me suspiciously.

"Yeah?" she said.

"Is Marvin here?" I asked.

"He's asleep," she said.

"Please wake him up," I said. "It's important."

When Maddy disappeared, I peeked inside the narrow strip of the apartment that I could see. The red sofa was torn and covered. Dirt, dust, and scattered newspapers covered the floor. I remembered that Marvin used to steal newspapers off the porches of people's houses and then sell them. I also heard that when he sold candy bars and raffle tickets, he kept the money. Once he stole a kid's shirt in school, and wore it the next day. When Molly found out and threatened to rip it off his back, stubborn Marvin stuck to his story that it was his. I had to make sure I didn't tick Marvin off. That would mean disaster.

The door creaked open. I smiled nervously as Marvin rubbed his sunken eyes. When he saw me, his eyes popped open.

"What's up, Marv?" I said with a smile, as if there was nothing strange about me stopping by his house at 7:30 in the morning.

"I'm still asleep," he grumbled. "What do you want, Penny?"

I looked down at the ground and took a deep breath. Then I picked my head up, and stared right into his eyes. "You know about how we were raising money to go to soccer camp, right?"

"Yeah," he said.

"Well, yesterday at the park, somebody took all our money," I said. "When word gets back to Mr. G, I'm in trouble. I was the one who was supposed to look after it. You wouldn't know who took it, would you?"

He shook his head. I took another deep breath.

"I had it in the lunch box and it was sitting right on the porch," I said. "Then I turned and ran down the alley. Who do you think could have gotten to it?"

He shrugged.

"Why would somebody take it?" I asked.

His eyes dropped to the ground. "Maybe they just needed it."

"For what?" I said. "To buy a pair of shoes? Jewelry? Something they really don't need?"

"Maybe for food and some clothes," he said.

I reached down to the ground and grabbed the brown bag. I lifted it up and handed it to him. Then I stuck my hand in my pocket and pulled out $10.

"Here's some money I won from some kid who thought he could beat me at the Summer Fest."

Marvin's guilty eyes shifted around the porch.

"Please, Marvin," I said as I held out the $10 bill. "I know you need money, too. I'll get my dad to help you work for some. But you've got to give our money back. It isn't right to be taking things from your friends."

When his sudden look of panic flashed into anger, a chill shot up my back. I had pressed him too far. I wanted so badly to take my words back and try it all over again. But it was too late.

Marvin gritted his teeth and shouted, "You're not my friend!"

He slammed the door shut in my face and I froze. I stood on his porch as I stared helplessly at the peeling paint on the front door. My eyes began to water. I was angry and sad. I wanted the money back so badly, but I had no idea what life was like behind that door. I couldn't understand him, so I didn't expect him to understand me. I set the grocery bag down and dropped my $10 inside. I walked down the steps and turned back to the house.

Maddy's wide eyes peeped from under the curtain. Then the curtain dropped, and she was gone.

It was a long, slow walk back to my house. I sat on my front porch alone for almost an hour trying to imagine how hard it was to live in Marvin's house. He never really had a childhood. Nobody ever gave him a chance.

I heard our front door creak open, but I did not turn around. My grandmother bent down and sat right next to me. She did not ask what had happened, she just waited for me to tell her. When I didn't speak, she knew that I had failed.

"You did your best, right?" she said.

I didn't move.

"You didn't yell or scream or shout at him. You asked him kindly. You treated him as a human being, didn't you?"

"I tried to," I said.

"You did more for him today than any other person has done in a long time," she said.

She rubbed my back with her soft hands. I looked into the distance, and spotted a barefoot little girl walking toward us. As she grew closer, I could see that it was Maddy. She jogged up to me and handed me an envelope.

"Marvin wanted me to give you this," she said.

I took the envelope and she ran away.

Chapter Nine

My grandmother, who had decided to stay for an extended visit, gave me two phone messages that week. She said some boy called twice and that he didn't leave his name. It had to be Cowboy. I'd seen him once at the park, so I didn't know what he could possibly want to talk to me about. Cowboy was cool, but calling me every day was crazy. I needed my space. Between playing ball, going to camp, and hanging out with my friends and family, I decided that I didn't have time for a relationship.

"When are you gonna tell him?" Molly asked after I explained it to her.

"One of these days I will," I said. "Maybe after camp."

"He'll figure it out by then," she said.

My grandmother made me take care of it sooner than I had hoped. The night before camp, she said to me, "You'd better call your little friend back."

"What?" I said. I didn't want to believe that she had really stuck her nose into my personal business.

"I'm not encouraging you to go running around with boys. But I don't care who it is — it's not right to think you cannot call a person back."

"I will," I muttered.

"Set him straight if you want, but let him hear it from you," she continued.

I didn't understand why she was putting so much importance on the issue. "I'm 12 years old," I pleaded.

"I don't care how old you are," she replied. "You always treat people with respect."

I huffed as my grandmother handed me the phone.

"May I please have some privacy?" I asked.

"No, you may not," she said.

I should have known better. Privacy was not in her dictionary when it came to family matters. I took a deep breath, picked up the phone and dialed. The phone rang six times.

"Nobody's home," I said and I hung up.

"Who are you calling?" my father said as he walked into the kitchen. "Better not be some kid named Cowboy."

He laughed and then grinned. I just shook my head and accepted that nothing was a secret in my house.

"Tell your father about Marvin," my grandmother muttered to me. "He will help him get a job."

"Who wants a job?" my dad asked.

I took another deep breath. The whole part of the story about Marvin was not what worried me. I didn't know what my father would say or do when he found out Mr. O'Malley never had the money. Maybe if I told him about Marvin taking the money, he wouldn't think much about my not telling him the entire story.

"Dad," I said. "I need to help Marvin."

"And why's that?" he said.

"The other day at the car wash, you asked where the money was," I began. "Molly told you that her father had it. Well, he didn't. Somebody took it."

My father froze, and then he turned to me.

"It was Marvin," I explained. "I didn't want to tell you because Mr. G told me to watch it, and I messed up."

"Where's the money, Penny?" he asked sternly.

"I got it back," I said. "Marvin didn't give it back right away. But after I talked to him, he sent his little sister to give it to me. I gave it to Ma, and she gave it to Mr. G."

"Let me get this straight," my father said. "You want me to help Marvin after he stole something from you and your friends?"

"I just feel bad because all of us are leaving for camp, and Marvin's got nothing to do. Everybody knows he steals. They make fun of him for it all the time."

"So how are you gonna help?"

"I thought maybe you could help Marvin," I said.

Aside from teaching special education classes, my father served as a mentor for many boys around the city. I picked up early on how fair my father was to others. He always gave every kid a chance.

"Can you find him a job?" I asked. "Maybe mowing lawns, washing cars, cleaning up? Or a paper route?"

"He can't get another paper route because of what he did last time he had one."

"There still has to be something," I pleaded.

"I'll see what I can do," he said. "But under one condition." Then he paused and looked right at me. "You've got to promise that you won't feel sorry for somebody who breaks the rules."

I nodded, thinking it was the end of our discussion. A sense of relief washed over me. I had found a way to help Marvin. I smiled proudly. But my father wasn't finished.

"And one more thing," he said, and then he paused. "Please don't lie to me again."

I looked to the ground in shame. My father was right. By not telling him the entire truth, I had lied.

"Sorry, Dad," I said.

After he accepted my apology, I moped to my bedroom. All the good feelings I had for helping out Marvin disappeared with that one disappointed look on my father's face.

•   •   •   •

The next morning my grandmother came in and woke me up five minutes before my alarm was set to go off. I groaned as I pulled the sheets over my head.

"Don't forget to write me while you're at camp," she said. "I want to know how you're doing."

I dragged myself out of bed and went into the kitchen where a full breakfast of pancakes, bacon, eggs, and biscuits awaited me. I ate every crumb, knowing it would be a week before I tasted another good meal. I wasn't the only one who was concerned about the food situation at soccer camp. Wil pushed her way through my front door with a medium-sized bag for her clothes, and a large bag stuffed with goodies and treats.

"I brought some food," she said.

"I can see that," I added.

Behind her came Molly, Angel, and Rosie.

"What time is Mr. G coming?" Molly asked.

"Eight," I said.

"I can't wait to get there!" Angel said.

"Who has been to this camp before?" I asked. "Don't they have a bunch of sports going on?"

"Yeah," Rosie said. "Rico went there once for a baseball camp."

"Boys are going to be there?" Angel asked.

Rosie nodded. Angel, who was famous for her cute outfits and bows, paid a little more attention to boys than the rest of us did. Ever since she turned 13, she had developed this habit of brushing her hair constantly. And whenever we were in a mixed crowd of boys and girls, Angel didn't talk as much as she used to.

"Why are you so worried about boys being there?" Molly asked.

"I'm not," Angel shot back.

Before it went any further, Rosie asked quietly, "Do you think they'll let us call home?"

"Yeah," Wil said. "What do you think it is? Prison?"

Rosie shrugged. I could tell that it was going to be a long week for Rosie to be away from Broadway Ave.

"Good morning," a voice called out and all eyes turned to the front door. Mr. G pulled off his shades as he stepped inside. My grandmother walked up to him with a cup of coffee. He reached out for the cup and nodded his thanks.

"Are you girls all packed and ready to go?" he said.

My little brother Sammy ran down the hall and right up to Mr. G. "Why can't I go?" he asked.

"When you're bigger," Mr. G said.

Sammy clicked his tongue. "I am bigger," he said.

"Come on, Shorty," I teased him. "Go get some breakfast."

He marched into the kitchen with a scowl on his face.

"Are there bats and mice in the cabins?" Wil asked.

"Lots," Mr. G said with a wide grin.

"Come on, Mr. G," Wil implored. "For real?"

"You'll be fine," he said. "There are cabins, a lake, a cafeteria, and a bunch of soccer fields. What else could you ask for?"

"How's the food?" Wil asked.

"Great," he said.

I never before heard anyone use "great" to describe camp food. It couldn't possibly be the truth.

"I'm even going to stay for lunch when I drop you girls off," Mr. G added.

I still didn't believe him.

We packed all our bags in Mr. G's truck and piled in for the two-hour ride. I wrestled my way into the front seat, which irked Molly and Wil. But after they took their seats in the back, Molly fell asleep within 15 minutes. Angel and Wil listened to Rosie's headphones, while Rosie read a baseball magazine. I looked down at the open road in front of us.

"I talked to a coach and told her all about you," Mr. G said to me. "She's going to teach you a couple of things that can improve your game. She played soccer at a big-time college."

I turned and stared blankly out the window. The last thing I wanted was more special attention. As much as Mr. G wanted to help, he didn't realize that this was my chance to get away. All I wanted to do was disappear to an unknown place and just play.

My eyes widened as we pulled into the main driveway of Bass Lake Camp. Red and white cabins sat among a bunch of trees along a road of dirt, stones, and roots. Girls of all ages lugged bags and suitcases.

"There's the office," Molly called out. "Over there where those girls are in line."

Mr. G pulled off to the side of the road. We jumped out of the van and I stretched out my tired, stiff body. Then Molly and Angel started pulling out the bags.

"Let's go!" Angel said.

"Wait up," I said. "Slow down."

"Sorry," Angel said. "I'm excited."

"I guess so," I mumbled.

We started to walk away, but Mr. G reached out and held me back. I turned and looked up into his dark sunglasses.

"Penny," he said in a serious tone. "I'm leaving you in charge of all the girls. If you need anything or there are any problems, call me at this number. I don't care what time. Keep everyone busy. And do as you're told."

He handed me a piece of paper. "Thanks, Mr. G." I said, accepting the responsibility.

We checked in and then walked toward our new home for the week: Cabin F. Wil skipped up the steps and stopped. By her wide eyes, I could tell that the thought of what was inside crossed her mind. I decided to play a trick on her as she apprehensively pushed on the light wooden door. It creaked as it swung open.

"AHHHHHH!" I screamed and pointed and jumped up and down. Wil flew down the stairs and clung onto me. Molly started screaming. Rosie and Angel darted away.

"What is it?" Molly called out.

Then I stopped, and laughed. "Just kidding," I said.

Everyone breathed a sigh of relief, as I kept laughing. Then Wil charged up to me.

"Real funny, P," Wil said as she smacked me on the arm. "That was not cool."

The rest of the Ballplayers saw the humor in what I'd done, and they started to giggle.

"That was good," Angel said. "You got all of us on that one."

We gathered ourselves together and walked back up the steps. Wil made me pull open the door this time. I reached out and did as she asked. Then we all stepped inside our new home.

"It's like we're sleeping outside," Wil said.

She had that right. Mattresses on bunks, a wooden floor and walls were the only thing that separated us from the ground, and from all the animals that crept around outside at night.

"I got the bed closest to the door," Wil announced.

"Why?" Angel said.

"Just in case I have to get outta here in a hurry," she said.

"Animals walk through the doors just like people," Molly said, wincing as she thought about it. "I'm on the top bunk by the door then."

"We've got to go to the cafeteria," Angel said. "Mr. G is waiting."

After we dropped our gear off, we walked outside and made our way to the cafeteria. I noticed a thick white line that was painted on the ground.

"What's that line for?" I asked.

Nobody answered. I walked up to Mr. G., and asked him the same question.

"It separates the two camps that are going on right now," he explained. "The boys at baseball camp are on one side, and you girls playing soccer are over here. You have to stay on your side or else."

"Or else what?" Wil said.

"I don't know for sure," he said firmly. "But you don't need to find out. There's no telling what Coach Oslo might do."

"Who's Coach Oslo?" Molly asked.

"He's the director," he said. "From what I hear, he's pretty tough."

As we walked into the dining room, Mr. G turned his attention to a young muscular woman in baggy shorts who was standing in line. The woman turned and smiled at Mr. G.

"Hey, Mr. Gordon!" she yelled as she started to walk over to us.

She reached out and gave him a hug.

"I'd like you to meet my girls here," Mr. G said. He went around and introduced all of us.

"This is Rita," Mr. G said.

"You girls all live on Broadway, right?" Rita asked.

"Yep," Molly said.

"I'm from the East Side," Rita added. "But I used to visit my cousins on Broadway. Do you play at the park?"

We all nodded proudly.

"Yeah," she said. "I used to play there, too."

The conversation turned back to Mr. G and Rita. We all stood around looking at each other. They talked for a while, and then Rita's eyes stopped on me.

"You're Penny, right?" she said. "I've heard a lot of good things about you."

I smiled nervously. Then my mind raced with worry. *Why did she have to say it in front of my friends?* I couldn't bear to look at Angel. Her favorite sport was soccer, and she was pretty good at it. It must have killed her to listen to praise from people who hadn't even seen me play. I dropped my head.

"Girls, have a seat for lunch," Mr. G said. "I've got some catching up to do with the coaches."

We all walked off together, and joined the dozens of girls filing into the cafeteria. When Wil saw that pizza was served for lunch, she couldn't stop smiling. One of the servers mumbled to me, "This is the best meal you'll get. So eat up."

I was glad the woman said it to me and not to Wil and Molly. Otherwise, Mr. G would have had company on the drive back to the city.

"Thanks," I said.

87

After lunch, we said good-bye to Mr. G on our way to the playing field.

"Be safe," he said.

"We know, Mr. G," I said. "We know."

Rita came up to us. "Have a seat girls," she said. "Coach Oslo has a lot of things to say."

We all sat down on the field, just as a muscular man with a tight white shirt and soccer shorts stepped in front of the group.

"Good afternoon, ladies," he said in a deep voice. "I'm Coach Oslo."

I could tell by his icy stare that he did not need to use the whistle around his neck. Wil leaned over me and the rest of the Ballplayers.

"Hey," she said. "I hear the best player at camp is a girl named Kara. I heard all the coaches talking about her."

"Excuse me!" Coach Oslo called out. His eyes were locked onto Wil. "Do you have something to say to the group?"

Wil shook her head nervously. All 120 girls were looking right at all of us. Molly nudged me in my side. Angel mumbled, "Uh-oh."

"What's your name?" Coach Oslo asked Wil.

"Wil," she muttered.

"Come on up here, and show us your push-ups," Wil said.

Wil's face dropped.

"Hurry up!" Coach Oslo said. "We don't talk when others are talking. That's a rule we have here. Your actions have consequences. Here is one consequence for talking when you're not supposed to."

This guy was serious. With Mr. G gone, we didn't have any adults to get Wil out of this mess.

She pushed herself up off the ground. As she hustled up to the front, she pulled her shirt over her snug shorts. I had been wishing for Coach Oslo to start laughing like it was all just a joke. But it wasn't.

"On the ground," he said. "Let's go."

Wil slumped to the ground, and stayed on her knees for a second. She looked up at us, and shook her head in anger and humiliation.

I stood up, jogged in front of camp and knelt down beside her. Molly, Angel, and Rosie followed right behind me.

"Hold it!" Coach Oslo said. "You can't have your friends bail you out of this one."

"We were talking, too, Coach Oslo," I said softly.

He stopped, looked up in the air pensively, and shook his head.

"Everybody down!" he said. Wil and Molly groaned and grunted as we all pumped out 10 push-ups. Then he ordered us to sit back down.

"I have some rules we need to discuss," he announced.

Coach Oslo didn't just have some rules. He had many. The last one on his list seemed to be the most important rule of them all.

"There's a line separating the boys' and girls' camps," he said firmly. "Do not cross that line. I repeat. Do not cross that line."

Many of the girls around us chuckled quietly. I smiled and shook my head, wondering why the man felt he had to paint an actual line on the ground.

"What's the big deal?" one girl muttered, and the girls around her shrugged.

I had a hunch that somebody was going to cross the line.

Chapter Ten

After the introduction, Rita stepped up and called out our station assignments. Within five minutes the whole camp was running around, trying to find six different places at once.

"See you later," I called out to my friends. When I jogged up to my station, I did not recognize any of the players.

"Hi, Penny," Rita called out in front of the group.

I looked up at her and smiled politely. All I could think about was how everyone noticed that Rita already knew my name.

"Come on up here, and demonstrate with me," she said.

I did as she asked only because I knew that Rita thought she was helping me. But she didn't realize that by singling me out so soon that all the other girls would think I enjoyed the attention. I didn't. I just wanted to be normal.

"Kara," Rita called out. "Come on up here and join us."

A thin girl with long stringy blonde hair and a tiny, round mouth stood along side of me. Out of the corner of my eye, I watched as she played with the soccer ball as if it were attached to her feet.

She did one fancy move, and I tried to do the same. I screwed up the first few times, and then I did it.

Kara and I battled in every station – throw-ins, corner kicks, fast break drills, and even the goalie drills. I tried to joke around with her a few times, and added a smile or laugh, but she was all business.

"Where you from?" I asked.

"Maplewood," she mumbled and then she looked into the distance.

I jogged away, and told myself that maybe she was just shy. In the next drill, Kara and I played each other one-against-one. I zipped around her and she elbowed me in the side. When Rita blew the whistle and gave me the ball, Kara glared at me. On the next play, I scored. Kara scowled and angrily stomped away.

By the time the last whistle blew, the muscles in my legs were burning. I walked over to the cafeteria not wanting to talk to anyone until I reached the water cooler. Two girls came up to my side.

"Hey, Penny," one said. "You're good."

I smiled and mumbled, "Thanks," as I reached down and grabbed a paper cup.

"Where are you sitting for dinner?" the other asked.

"I'm waiting for my friends," I said.

"We're waiting for one of our friends, too. Do you know Crazy Candi?"

I shook my head. Then a girl with bleached yellow hair came skipping up to us.

"What-up-what-up-what-up?" she called out.

I shrugged, not knowing what to say to this energetic person.

"Who are you?" she asked me.

"Penny."

"Well, you are lucky to know me," she said as she laughed. "What cabin are you in?"

"F," I replied.

"We're in K," she said. "K is for Koo-koo. And my nickname is Crazy Candi, 'cause that's what I am. Crazy!"

I laughed as we walked into the dining hall together. I could tell right away that she was not kidding about being crazy. Candi seemed like she could keep everyone laughing.

"Sit with us, Penny," Candi called out.

"I'm going to sit over there with my friends," I replied.

"Fine," she said as I walked away. "Be like that."

"There's not enough room for all three of you," I explained.

"Catch you later, P," Candi called out.

I picked up my tray of food, and sat down at the table between Angel and Rosie. Molly's sunburned cheeks looked hot. Wil took off her glasses and set them on the table. She took a napkin and blotted her face dry. Wil eyed the new girls I had met, and asked, "Who are they?"

"I don't know," I said.

"You meet that girl Kara yet?" Angel said.

"Somebody said all the coaches love her but she's a real snob," Molly said. "She doesn't talk to anybody."

"That doesn't mean anything," Rosie said defensively.

Rosie Jones was a girl of little words. Her brow furrowed whenever anybody made fun of her for being shy. One of her best lines she used was when an obnoxious kid kept trying to get her to talk. She looked at him square in the eyes and said, "I don't go around telling you to shut up, do I?" The boy never bothered Rosie again.

"Kara's good," I said. "She's in my station group."

"Is she nice?" Wil asked.

"She hasn't said much," I replied, "so I don't know."

Rosie nodded her head in agreement. Then she took a bite out of her hamburger.

"How was your group?" I asked Rosie.

She shrugged. That meant it was OK. For the moment everything seemed fine for Rosie. Once I had been with my cousin Jackie when Rosie flipped out and wanted to go home. One minute she was fine, and the next she was hysterical. I kept my fingers crossed that Rosie would keep herself together.

After dinner, we were split up into teams. When I found out Rosie was on my team, I gave her a high five. Then I looked over my shoulder. The two girls I had met earlier were right next to us.

"What's up, P?" one said. "Take it easy on us this game."

I couldn't figure out what was going on. I'd never seen them before in my life. They seemed nice, but they were acting a little too strange for me.

"I'm Jules, and this is Lucy."

"This is my friend, Rosie," I said. "She's from my neighborhood."

Jules and Lucy smiled at Rosie. Rosie gave them a long, distrustful stare.

"Let's go, girls," Rita called out. "I asked to coach your team, Penny," she whispered.

Great. Just great. Why can't I just be normal? Why did everyone always give me so much special attention?

At the end of the last session of drills, we all met on the main field. Coach Oslo gave us the next day's schedule, and then he called out an announcement about a special award that was given out each day. As he started to speak, my mind drifted to calculating how many hours of sleep I would get that night.

"The player of the day is Penny Harris!" he said.

The next thing I knew was I was being pushed up in front of the entire camp to collect my special T-shirt. I looked up into the crowd, and saw one girl frowning.

It was Kara. She looked at me, and then walked away.

Chapter Eleven

After Coach Oslo handed me my T-shirt, I smiled at the crowd that had gathered around me.

"Player of the Day," one coach called out. "Soon to be Player of the Year!"

I tried to get mad, but I couldn't. So I just kept smiling. Nobody would understand why a kid would be mad about being so good at something. I turned to my friends, who had been waiting. And waiting.

"I'm hungry," Wil moaned.

"I'm tired," Rosie said.

"My feet hurt," Angel grumbled. "I'm walking back."

"Come on, P," Molly moaned. "You take forever sometimes."

They started to walk away. I ran away from the coaches and players, and jogged to catch up with my friends.

"Wait up!" I called out.

"We did," Molly said.

"Sorry," I muttered.

"My feet are killing me," Angel moaned.

"It's from all that running you do," Wil said. "You don't see my feet with bunions and calluses and warts all over them do you?"

"I don't have warts," Angel said.

"After we get through in those gross showers, we all might," Molly said.

"Lemme see your T-shirt, P," Rosie said.

I hesitated in fear of my friends thinking that I was showing off.

"Hold it up so we all can see," Angel said.

I held it up across my chest.

"It's cool," Molly said.

"Yeah," Rosie said.

"And they said that Kara was the best," Wil added. "Yeah, right."

"Kara's different," Molly said. "She has her nose stuck up in the air all the time."

"She's just quiet," I told her. "She's all right."

We walked up the steps to our cabin. When Molly flicked on the light, I looked into the bed next to me. A lump was under the covers.

"Who's sleeping already?" Wil said.

I walked closer and bent over to check out our bunkmate. The girl turned over and she opened her eyes. It was Kara. She looked right at me and then ducked her head under her blanket.

"Let's be quiet," I said. "She looks tired."

We tiptoed around trying to keep the noise down. Molly stubbed her toe, screamed, and we all burst out laughing.

"What's going on?" a voice yelled from the front door. We turned and watched Candi push open our cabin door.

"Shhhh!" I said. "Kara's asleep."

We all turned to Kara. She did not move. I took a deep breath, and looked at Candi. I could tell by her devilish smile that she was up to something.

"I'll give $10 to the person who crosses the white line," she said.

"I'll do it," Molly said.

"Would you use your head before you go jumping into things?" Wil asked. She punched Molly in the shoulder and then turned back to Candi. "How far does she have to cross?"

"Just far enough to write 'Losers' on the door with whipped cream."

"That's far," Angel said. "And I wouldn't want Coach Oslo catching me."

Molly looked at Candi and asked, "Why don't you do it?"

"I've already done it," she said. "It's easy."

If Candi already did it, then the boys would be ready to retaliate, and knowing Molly, she'd probably trip, fall, and crawl back in the mud. Then she'd get caught.

"Molly," I said firmly. "Don't do it."

Molly turned back to Candi, and said, "Twenty bucks."

"No," I called out. "You're not doing it. I told Mr. G none of us would get in trouble. You're not doing it."

Then an object bounced off our screen. We all turned to the window.

"What was that?" Rosie asked. "It's the boys throwing tennis balls," Candi said. "We've got to get them back."

From under the covers, Kara huffed loudly and groaned.

"Keep it down," I said.

"Fine," Candi asked. "What's her problem?"

"Nothin'," I said. "She's just tired. We're going to bed."

"Lights out in 10 minutes!" Coach Oslo called out. "Let's go, girls!"

"I'm not doing any more push-ups," Wil said nervously. "Let's get to bed."

97

Candi walked toward the door. "Tomorrow night, we're doing it," she said.

We stayed up for about an hour, laughing, and joking around. Then I heard a scraping on the wall.

"Shhh," I said, and the cabin fell silent. The scraping on the wood grew louder.

"What's that?" she yelled.

Everyone stopped and listened to the noise again.

"It's probably just Candi foolin' around," I said.

Then we heard it again.

"It's the boys," Molly said.

Nobody said a word for another five seconds. Rosie's wide eyes turned to me.

"Is somebody out there?" she asked.

"Go look, Penny." Wil said.

"Why me?" I asked.

"Because you're the player of the day," she said.

Angel added, "Yeah, P. You go."

I huffed as I stood up. Then I tiptoed over to the window with my flashlight in hand. I took a deep breath and flicked the light on. Something rustled the bushes. Then everything was still.

"It's nothing," I said as I quickly crawled back into my bed.

"Candi said something earlier about some Hookman," Wil said. "He walks around at night and scares kids with a hook. I guess he lost his hand doing something."

"She's crazy," Angel said. "Don't believe her."

"Shhhh," I said. "Kara's sleeping."

"So?" Wil said. "It's the first night. We're supposed to stay up late."

Either Wil stopped talking or we stopped listening. I don't know which came first. The last thing I remembered hearing was Wil telling the story about how her cousin was at a camp where there really was a scary guy wandering around at night. Eventually everyone dozed off.

When I woke up the next morning, I thought I was in an icebox. I reached into my bag and put on my sweatshirt. I got up to go to the bathroom, and turned right into Kara.

"Hi," I said.

She mumbled a greeting, and then headed right toward her bunk. I went to the sink and brushed my teeth. We all left the cabin at the same time, including Kara. When we reached the cafeteria, I turned to ask Kara if she wanted to eat with us. But she was gone.

"Where'd Kara go?" I asked.

"We don't know," Wil said. "She hasn't said a word to any one of us."

"Maybe she wants to go home," Rosie suggested.

"She must not like us," Wil added.

"Well, if you weren't talking so much last night maybe she would," Molly said.

"Oh, and it's now my fault?" Wil asked.

"It's nobody's fault," I said. "That's just the way she is."

After we went through the breakfast line, Candi, Jules, and Lucy sat down at our table.

"Did anyone hear the Hookman last night?" Candi asked.

None of us said a word. We didn't want to admit to anything.

"We did," Jules said. "Lucy almost wet her pants she was so scared."

Molly stopped eating. Rosie's mouth dropped open.

"I told you, Penny," Wil said as she turned to me. "I told you."

"It was you, wasn't it?" I asked Candi.

"No way," she said as she checked over each of her shoulders. "I don't joke about the Hookman." She lowered her voice to a whisper. "He wanders around in his ugly purple collared shirt and gray sweat pants. This guy is nuts."

"It's the boys," Molly said.

"Trust me," Candi said. "It's not."

The next thing I knew we were out of the cafeteria and jogging, stretching, and running to our stations. My legs ached. My body craved for sleep. But with Kara in my group, I had no time to rest. We competed at everything we did. Passing. Heading. Dribbling. During a fast-break drill, I fell down. I turned over, looked up and reached out to an extended hand. I jumped up, and came eye to eye with the person who had helped me on my feet again. It was Kara.

"Thanks," I said.

Kara said nothing as we walked back to the water cooler with the rest of the girls from my station.

"What up, Sweet P?" Candi called out and she came running at us. "You two going to lunch?"

"In a minute," I said.

"You're in on the tennis ball fight later, aren't you?" she asked.

I stopped and thought for a second before I answered. *Why did she care about me being in the tennis ball fight? Did it matter that much? Why did she need me in on it?*

Before I said anything, Candi turned to Kara and said, "You're in too, aren't you?"Kara turned to me and shrugged. "I guess," she said.

Angel and Molly jogged up to us.

"I got hit in the face," Molly said proudly.

She turned her left cheek so I could see. Sure enough, she had the faint imprint of a soccer ball pressed into her skin. I shook my head. Only Molly would go around telling people she got smacked in the face. My father had nicknamed her "Bull" because she crashed and banged herself around, just like a bull in a china shop. Each bruise in her collection had a special story behind it.

"Can you see it?" she asked.

"Yeah," I said.

"Who kicked it?" Candi asked.

"I did," Angel said softly. "I'm sorry, Molly. I'm really sorry. I didn't mean it."

"Don't worry about it," Molly said, and then she turned to me. "I got the save."

We walked into the cafeteria. Jules and Lucy were already sitting at our usual table. Kara was standing by herself in line. I walked up to her and asked, "You wanna sit with us?"

She nodded. We walked over to our table, which was already full.

"Would you scoot down a bit?" Wil asked.

Jules and Lucy squeezed together.

"Who's going swimming after lunch?" Lucy asked.

All the Ballplayers were, except me. I didn't swim. My muscles tightened up whenever I came within 50 feet of water.

"You're paranoid," Molly said.

I smiled as I shook my head.

"Call it what you want, but I'm not putting my big toe in that dirty lake," I said.

"It's not dirty," Molly said.

While the others followed the path down to the beach, I went to one of the fields. I ran kicking my soccer ball, eager to find some peace and quiet. When I looked up at the field, I slowed down. A player was already there. It was Kara. She looked up at me, then she looked back down at the ball. I nudged the ball with my toe and kept moving right toward her.

"How come you're not swimming?" I asked.

She shrugged. "How come you're not?"

"I can't swim," I said.

Kara's face lit up.

"Me neither," she said.

She smiled, and so did I. It actually felt good to be really bad at something that came easy to everyone else. Kara and I continued talking as if we'd known each other for a long time.

"Do you believe the Hookman story?" she asked me.

I hesitated. I didn't know if I could trust Kara enough to tell her about what I saw in the bushes. If word got back to Wil and Rosie, they'd be on the next ride out of Bass Lake Camp and back to Broadway Ave.

"Did you hear the scraping last night?" I asked.

She nodded her head.

"I thought you were asleep," I said.

"No," Kara said. "I heard it all."

"When I went to the window, I saw something move," I said.

Kara sucked in air. "You did?"

"I bet it was Candi foolin' around," I said, "or some raccoon."

Kara wasn't so sure. "I don't know, Penny," she said. "I heard a bunch of girls talking about the Hookman today. What if there really is some crazy guy out there?"

I didn't answer. My attention turned to Wil, Molly, Rosie, and Angel, who were walking up the hill and were heading for our cabin. Kara and I jogged over to them.

"How was your swim?" I asked.

"It was fine when I wasn't drowning," Molly grumbled.

"What?" I asked.

"Candi went around dunking and splashing all of us," Wil said bitterly. "That girl is wild."

Kara and I waited for them to change into their clothes, and then we all walked down to the main field for more drills and our afternoon game.

"What's up, P?" Rita asked as we passed her. I mumbled hello and smiled. Despite my being with a group of players, she only said hi to me.

"We're playing the Stars this afternoon," Rita said.

"That's our team," Molly said and she turned to Angel.

As many times as we played against each other at the park, I never really liked playing against my friends at any other time. By the time the game started, I had made up my mind that I wasn't going to show up my friends. Rita blew the whistle and called us in. Rosie and I huddled up with the rest of our team.

"We've got to keep it spread out and get the ball to Penny in the middle," Rita said. "Get it to Penny."

All eyes fell on me. Most of my teammates were all smiles, but even I got tired of how much Rita and Coach Oslo talked about me.

I dogged it through the first five minutes of the game. My two teammates, Debbie and Lisa, controlled the ball and took the shots on goal. Molly was keeper, and she made every save. Everyone seemed happy. Well, almost everyone.

"PENNY!" Rita screamed at me. "GET YOUR HEAD IN THE GAME!"

I started running a little faster.

"We need you to score!" Rita screamed. "Get the ball and take some shots!"

I nodded my head and did as I was told. Rosie kicked me a sweet pass and I headed it right past Molly and into the goal. Molly punched the ground in disgust, as Rosie ran up and gave me five. But Rosie was the only one on my team who congratulated me. All of our other teammates just returned to their positions. Five minutes later, I scored again.

"Nice shot," Angel said.

Rita clapped, too. The rest of my teammates stood around for a second. Debbie clicked her tongue. Lisa rolled her eyes. The next time I got the ball, they all muttered, "Pass!" or "Over here!" Debbie wanted the ball. Lisa wanted the ball. Everybody wanted the ball. But there was only one ball.

When the game was over, I walked off the field by myself trying to think of some way to keep everyone happy.

Chapter Twelve

As I began to pick at my plate of food later that night, I felt a tap on my shoulder.

"Penny," Denise asked. "Can we sit with you?"

I looked up at Denise and Lisa, and hesitated. "Yeah," I said. "Sure."

Molly and Wil slid over on the bench to make just enough room for Lisa between them. Jules and Kara did the same for Denise.

"Did you hear or see the Hookman around yet?" Candi asked Denise.

"No," she replied. "Who's the Hookman?"

Candi's mouth dropped open. "You mean to tell me you don't know?"

Lisa and Denise looked at each other and shrugged.

"He's the crazy man in the purple shirt and gray sweat pants who wanders around at night," Candi explained.

"The guy's got a hook instead of a hand," Wil added.

I looked at her and wondered how somebody so smart could believe such a bad story. I laughed as I shook my head. She turned to me and said, "I've read about guys like the Hookman."

"You read too many scary books, Wil," Angel said.

Molly and Rosie didn't jump to either side of the story, which meant that they believed Candi's version, too. When I went up to get a drink, Coach Oslo called me over to the table where all the coaches were sitting. My nerves tingled as I walked over. I didn't want him to embarrass me.

"You're doing a nice job," he said. "Keep it up and you'll be a big-time player one day."

I just nodded as I walked away.

After dinner, Angel, Molly, and Rosie spent their free time down at the beach so Angel could soak her sore feet in the water. The rest of us hung out in our cabin. Wil was lying in her bed, while Kara and I sat up talking. Then Jules burst through the door.

"What are you doing?" she asked.

"Nothin'," I replied.

"Come over and hang out with us," she said.

"I don't know," I mumbled.

"Come on, P," Jules pleaded. "You're no fun."

I stopped before I said another word. *Maybe I wasn't any fun. Maybe I was too caught up in taking care of everyone else and doing the right thing.* I looked at Kara and Wil. Kara nodded and said, "Let's go."

"I'm tired," Wil added. "I'm going to take a nap. Penny, will you wake me up in 20 minutes?"

"Yeah," I said.

Kara and I walked out the door, and followed Jules into her cabin.

"What's up?" Candi called out.

A group of girls were huddled around Candi's bed.

"You want some?" she asked.

As Kara and I moved closer, my eyes grew wide at the huge stash of chocolate bars, jelly beans, hard candy, mints, and lollipops.

"They don't call me Candi for nothin'," she added with a smile.

All the girls around her dug in and helped themselves. I reached in and lifted up the stack of candy bars. As I reached down to the bottom, I peeked in and saw something I didn't want to see. A pack of cigarettes. I dropped it and then tried to quickly stuff it away.

Thump. We all turned toward the wall. *Thump-thump.*

"It's the boys again!" Jules called out, and everyone jumped up.

"We're on!" Candi announced.

She pulled out a suitcase full of tennis balls from underneath her bed. One by one all the girls in the cabin grinned devilishly as they grabbed three and four tennis balls apiece. Even Kara bent over to get hers. I was smiling and laughing along with everyone else. But just before I reached into the suitcase, I hesitated.

"Come on, Penny," Candi said. "Have some fun for once. We're not going to get in trouble. It's no big deal."

She was right. I was being no fun again. I reached in and grabbed as many as I could and flew out the door. We split into three different directions, tiptoed around the corners and hid in the bushes. Within seconds, tennis balls were flying all over the place, and everyone was laughing like crazy. Kara wound up and nailed one boy right in the chest. Candi jumped out of the bushes, got a running start, and chased another kid half her size down a path. I laughed as we all ran around. I wished the Ballplayers had been there. It was good clean fun until Candi raced across the white line.

"Uh-oh," Kara muttered.

Candi kept going. When she slipped into the boys' cabin, the rest of us watched quietly, and waited for her to come out.

"Coach Oslo is coming up the hill!" Lucy yelled. "Get outta here!"

I split out of there so fast that I didn't even remember running. The next thing I knew I was pushing through the front door of Cabin F and seeing Wil jump straight up out of her bed.

"What?" she screamed. "What? What is it?"

I stopped and took a deep breath.

"Nothin'," I breathed. "You gotta get up," I told her. "It's time to go."

Wil moaned and then pulled herself up. "You scared the life out of me, Penny. What were you doing?"

"Kara and I were just hanging out in Candi's cabin."

I didn't want to tell one of my closest friends that I was having fun without her. Then my mind raced with fear. *Where was Kara? Did she get caught by Coach Oslo? Was she OK?* The door creaked open. I turned eager to see Kara. But Molly, Angel, and Rosie were the only ones who walked in.

"Have you seen Kara?" I asked.

"Yeah," Angel said. "She's down at the main field."

"Is she in trouble?" I asked.

"No," Molly said. "Why would she be?"

I shrugged. I didn't want the Ballplayers to know what I'd done because I thought they would be mad for not including them in on the fun. We left the cabin together and headed down the path. Candi came running up to me as we approached the field.

"Wasn't that fun?" she said laughing.

I shrugged it off and kept walking as the rest of my friends eyed me suspiciously. Jules and Lucy ran over next to us.

"Coach Oslo almost caught Kara," Lucy whispered loudly to me, "but she got away."

"He wouldn't have done anything," Jules added. "We weren't doing anything bad. Kara's one of the best players here. He wouldn't punish her."

I stopped and thought about whether or not there was any truth in what she just had said. I wondered if Coach Oslo would be more lenient with the better players.

"What'd you do, Penny?" Molly blurted out impatiently.

The whistle blew.

"I'll tell you later," I muttered.

Our attention turned to Coach Oslo for our evening instructions. He gave them to us, and then added, "For your information, whoever was in on the tennis ball fight with the boys, you'd better not even think of doing it again."

Candi turned and looked at me with a crazy, sneaky smile. Then she burst out laughing. My eyes searched around for Kara. She turned to me and grinned, too.

But Molly and Wil were not smiling.

"Penny," Lucy whispered.

I turned as Lucy tossed a tiny rock at me. I caught it and threw it back at her with a grin. I turned back to Molly. My best friend would not look at me.

• • • •

We played three games that night. Coach Oslo watched me closely in every minute of the last two. I

109

tried to pretend he wasn't there or that he wasn't watching me — but I knew that he was.

We played our last game against Jules and Candi's team. It was hard to keep a straight face around the two of them. On one play, Jules' tripped and fell flat on her face. Everyone stopped and gasped, except for Candi. She burst out laughing, and then she imitated the same exact move, trip and fall.

"Did you have a nice trip, Jules?" she called out.

Later while I was cracking up at Candi again, I glanced over to the sidelines and spotted Coach Oslo. I stopped laughing, and finally started playing hard.

Rita screamed from the sidelines, "Get it to the middle! Get it to Penny!"

That meant for me to shoot. I did as I was asked. When I scored two goals in a row, Candi started boasting about me.

"You can't touch her," she called out from her spot in goal. "Somebody, anybody, everybody, mark Penny!"

The whistle blew and it was over. We won. I started to walk over to the water fountain.

"Penny!" Jules called out. "Come here for a sec."

I jogged over to Jules, Lucy and Candi.

"Do you wanna play on our four-on-four team?" Candi asked.

I thought of the Ballplayers. "I don't know," I said.

"It will be the three of us, Kara, and Lucy," Candi explained. "We get one sub."

"I'll be playing with my friends," I said.

"We're not your friends?" she asked.

"Yeah," I replied, "but I always play with the Ballplayers."

Lucy came running up to us. "Are you playing with us?" I shook my head.

"I told Molly and Wil and they said they didn't care at all," she said. "They already have their team."

My mind raced with questions. *Maybe the Ballplayers were mad at me for not spending as much time with them as I should have been. Maybe they went out and asked someone else to play with them. Would they do that to me?*

"What do you say, P?" Candi asked.

"I'll let you know later," I said as I jogged out on the field to kick the ball around by myself. I needed to be alone to think things through.

The rest of the players in camp milled around the field. After a few minutes, Coach Oslo blew the whistle, and we huddled up at center field. He made some announcements, and then called out the player of the day. It was Kara. She walked up to him. She grinned as she hustled back to her seat. All of Cabin F rooted wildly for her.

"Yeah, Kara!" I yelled.

Then Coach Oslo started calling out for us to hustle back into our cabins. Kara came up to me and said, "Are you ready to go?"

I nodded my head and wondered where the Ballplayers could be. *Why didn't they wait for me?* I started to worry again about them not wanting me to be around. As Kara and I were walking through the darkness, I heard a scream. An awful, loud, scared-to-death scream. It had to be Wil. I started running. When I reached the sight of the commotion, I pushed through the crowd.

"What happened?" I turned and asked Angel.

"We were walking along the path when we heard somebody chasing us. So we started running and then this guy jumped out at us. But it wasn't really a guy."

I turned and looked at a large stuffed animal that was dressed in a purple collared shirt and gray sweat pants.

"It was so funny, Penny!" Candi called out. "You should have seen the look on Wil's face when I threw this thing out of the tree."

Everyone started to crack up again. Lucy and Jules were in on it, too. I turned to Wil. She tried to smile, but I could tell she wasn't happy about what had happened. Molly scowled, and Rosie glared at Candi.

"Let's go," Angel said.

All of us walked back to Cabin F in silence. When we got into the cabin, everyone started talking with each other, but nobody would look at me.

"What's wrong?" I asked.

"What's wrong with us?" Molly asked.

"What?" I said.

"How come you won't play in the four-on-four tournament with us?"

"I never said that," I said. "Lucy came up and told me that you already had your own team, and that you didn't care if I played with them."

"We wouldn't say that!" Molly's voice cracked. "How could you believe that?"

"How could you think that I wouldn't want to play with you?" I asked.

"Candi is trouble, Penny," Wil said firmly.

"No she's not," I said defensively. "They just wanted me to play with them. They didn't plan any of this."

"Yeah, they did," Wil shot back.

Wil was still upset just because Candi played a joke on her. Molly was mad because Candi dunked her at the beach. I turned to Rosie. Rosie didn't say anything. I assumed that she wasn't too fond of Candi for one obvious reason. Candi was loud and Rosie was quiet. I turned to Angel, hoping that she would do like she normally does and point out the good things about everyone. She said nothing.

"There's nothing wrong with Candi," I stated firmly. "She's just fun. Isn't she Kara?"

Kara muttered, "Yeah, I guess."

"She's always kidding around," I explained with a smile.

When no one responded, I dropped the subject.

"So are we playing together tomorrow or what?" I asked.

Molly kept her stubborn head down. Wil climbed under her covers. Angel took a deep breath. Rosie looked up at me, shrugged her shoulders, and said firmly, "We'd better or else I'm going home."

Everyone burst out laughing at Rosie, and I breathed a sigh of relief. Then I thought of something that had slipped our minds. *What team was Kara going to be on?* We were her closest friends. She didn't talk to anyone else.

"How many players are we allowed on each team?" I asked.

"Five," Angel said. "We get one sub."

I turned to Kara as she slipped under her sleeping bag.

"Whose team are you going to play on?" I asked.

She shrugged. "Candi and Jules want me to play with them."

"Are you going to?" Molly asked.

"Yeah," she said, "I guess. They're the only other players I know."

"I'm sorry you can't play with us," I said. "I wish you could."

"Me too," Angel added.

"That's all right," Kara said.

Coach Oslo shouted from outside, "Lights out, Cabin F!"

I hustled to my bed as Molly flicked the switch.

"Oh no!" I said.

"What's wrong, P?" Molly asked.

"I was supposed to write my grandma," I said. "I'll do it tomorrow." Little did I know what a mess I would get myself into the next day.

Chapter Thirteen

Molly and I jogged down the path the next morning on the way to breakfast. We ran right into Coach Oslo at the bottom of the hill.

"Hi, Penny," he said.

I waited for him to greet Molly, but he didn't.

"What four-on-four team are you on?" he asked me. "I'll be sure to watch."

He pulled his clipboard up from his waist and had his pen ready.

"I'm playing with Molly, Wil, Rosie, and Angel," I said.

"Who was your fifth player again?" he asked as he scribbled down the names.

"Angel," I said.

"Oh yeah," he muttered. "Angel."

Molly looked at me and rolled her eyes. I looked at her and shrugged. We had been there for three days. Mr. G had introduced all of us to him. *How could Coach Oslo not know all of our names?*

"Your team doesn't need a sub," Coach Oslo said to me. "You count as two people."

He smiled. I didn't. *Did he honestly think that saying all these things now would make me want to play for his college someday?* He was crazy to think I was that dumb.

"What's your team name?" he asked.

"The Ballplayers," Molly said.

"Where'd you get that name?" he asked.

"It's from our neighborhood," Molly explained.

"Oh," he mumbled, and then he walked away without saying good-bye.

After our warm-up and stations, we jumped right into the first game of our four-on-four tournament.

"Who are we playing?" Angel asked.

"The Jazz," I replied.

"Who's on that team?"

"Denise and Lisa," I said.

I grinned. Their scoffs and snickers were tough to forget. Even Angel had picked up on their jealousy.

"Let's make 'em pay!" she said with a grin.

Molly started in her usual spot as keeper. Wil played fullback. Rosie, Angel, and I rotated in on the line. When the whistle blew, we began to move up and down the floor like a team. It was just like basketball. Just like softball. Just like we were at Anderson Park.

I pushed the ball to Angel, she wound up and took a shot. It was good.

"Yeah! Yeah! Yeah!" I screamed.

Denise and Lisa scowled as they walked past me. I ran over to Angel and slapped her five.

"Subs!" a coach shouted.

"I'll go out," I said.

"No, don't!" Angel said. "We need you, Penny."

The rules said that everyone must get equal playing time. I didn't want to cheat to win.

"I'll be right back in," I assured her. "I need a drink."

After I told Rosie she was in for me, I walked over to the cooler by myself.

"Hey!" Rita called out. "What's up, Sweet P?"

"Hi," I said.

"The counselors are playing later tonight," she said. "Do you want to play with us?"

"Who else is playing?" I asked.

"Just you and maybe Kara," Rita said. "What do you say?"I shook my head.

"What's wrong?" she asked.

"I don't want to play," I said.

"Why not?" Rita asked. She sounded mad at me, but I didn't care. "You're the best player here," she added.

I rolled my eyes. Rita had it all wrong. I was not the best player there. If Kara talked more, smiled and didn't mind people clinging to her all the time, Rita would be telling Kara this instead of me.

"I just don't want to," I repeated.

"You'll be fine," Rita told me. "I'll tell Coach Oslo that you're in."

As she walked away, I opened my mouth, but nothing came out. Rita had ignored every word I had said. She wanted me to play more than I did.

"Penny!" Molly screamed. I turned to her. She waved her hand and muttered, "Get back in, would ya?"

I huffed and nodded. There was no sense standing around worrying about everything. During a break in the action, I ran back onto the field.

"Come in for me!" Wil shouted.

I jogged out and stood by Molly for a few minutes.

"What's the score?" I said.

"Three to one," she said.

"How much time is left?"

"About 10 minutes," Molly replied.

Angel screamed, "Cover the middle of the field, Penny! We need you."

I charged up the field, but didn't go too deep. I couldn't leave Molly alone. As fun as it was to score, I accepted my job on defense, and refused to leave my keeper. Denise picked the ball from Rosie and then booted it over to Lisa. Within seconds, the game had changed momentum. Everyone was heading right toward me, and right toward Molly.

"Stop her, P!" Molly screamed.

I charged ahead and locked my eyes on the ball. At just the right minute, I jumped forward, stole the ball away from Denise, and then booted it up to Angel.

"Way to play, P!" Molly hollered. Her voice was hoarse, and her face was red. Even though we didn't talk about it, Molly also saw how Denise and Lisa acted around me. On the next play, I took the ball away from Lisa. I accidentally bumped her with my elbow as I did it.

"What was that?" Denise hollered as she turned to Rita. "Oh yeah, I forgot she's Penny. She's everybody's favorite."

My blood boiled. She spoke loud enough for everyone on the field and the sidelines to hear. My insides tightened up. I wanted to scream. But I held it all inside. Molly didn't.

"Shut up, Denise, and just play!" Molly hollered. "You're just jealous."

"No, I'm not!" Denise shot back.

I wanted to scream at Molly for mouthing off, but I didn't want to embarrass myself any further. I ran around the field, playing harder and harder with each step. The ball rolled toward me, and Lisa ran up to take it away. I threw a fake, dipped around her and kicked the ball ahead to Rosie.

"Ugh!" Lisa screamed. "Would somebody help me?"

The final whistle sounded, and we collected our first win. We went to slap everyone five. My glaring eyes warned Molly not to say a word to Denise or Lisa. She clicked her tongue, and muttered, "Don't worry about it."

The coaches huddled us up at center field and told us the schedule of events for the rest of the day and the evening.

"The counselors scrimmage tonight," Rita said.

"Can we play?" Denise asked.

"It's for coaches and a few players," Rita said.

"Who gets to play?" Lisa asked.

"Penny," Rita said.

All eyes fell on me. I shrugged my shoulders at Molly and muttered, "She told me I had to play." My eyes turned back to Rita. I couldn't go through this alone.

"What about Kara?" I asked.

"Yeah," Rita said. "Kara's in, too. I'll talk to the coaches later to see who else they're putting on the roster."

After Rita dismissed everyone, I jogged up alongside of her, determined to set things straight.

"Why don't you let everyone play?" I asked.

"There are too many campers," she said.

"Even if everyone only gets to play for two minutes," I said, "it's better than nothing."

Rita huffed. "I don't see why you're making such a fuss about it."

"Please?" I asked.

"I'll talk to Coach Oslo."

• • • •

After dinner, we split up and jogged over to our fields for an 11-on-11 game. With tomorrow being the last day of camp, we had to win in order to advance.

Denise and Lisa were in rare form from the start of the game.

"I was open," Lisa told me.

I nodded.

"Kick it to me down the sideline," Denise said. "We've got to keep it spread out."

"All right," I muttered as I kept running.

Somehow, we managed to win the game. No one would have ever guessed that we were undefeated by the way we treated each other that game. We all huddled around the water cooler, and listened as Denise called out everyone's individual statistics for the week.

"I've scored three times," Denise said after the game. "Lisa's scored four times. And Penny's scored something like nine times. You're so good, Penny. I wish I could score as much as you."

What? It didn't get any phonier than this. Lisa acted like my best friend in front of me, and then was my biggest critic behind my back. I really tried to get mad, and I did. But it only lasted about 30 seconds.

When Kara jogged up next to me, I joked around with her and forgot all about what Denise and Lisa were up to. As we approached the main field, Coach Oslo called out instructions.

"What are we playing now?" I asked.

"The Olympics," Kara said. "This is fun!"

"Two cabins per team!" Coach Oslo called out.

Out of nowhere, Jules and Lucy came running over.

"You wanna play with us?" Lucy asked.

I looked around. Wil looked down and Angel turned away. *What was everyone so worried about? Why couldn't everyone just get along and play together.?*

"Yeah," I said.

Everyone immediately started calling out their favorite events.

"I want to do the heading competition," Jules said.

"I wanted to do that," Angel replied.

"I'm doing the goalie drill," Molly said.

"You're always doing the keeper drills," Lucy replied. "Let somebody else for once."

"Hold up!" I said. "How are we ever going to win if we're already arguing?"

I took a loud breath, and then spoke softly and clearly. "Molly gets to do the keeper drills because she's good at them. Wil should kick in the long-ball competition 'cause she's a fullback. Rosie's in the dribbling drill. Candi's the best juggler. Angel can head the ball better than anyone here. Kara's the best scorer. Lucy's a great defensive player. She should do the defensive drill. Jules, you should do the throw-in. You're good at that. I've seen you throw it far."

As I called out everyone's names and told them why we needed them, they all nodded and agreed.

No longer were they thinking about themselves. They were thinking about what was best for the team. We all broke up into our groups. Within twenty minutes, everyone completed her event, raced back to the table and recorded the score. That was everyone except me. Just like in the double Dutch competition, I was last again. Dead last.

"It's all tied up, P" Molly said. "It's you against Denise for the last points to win."

I smiled as if finishing everything was my job on earth.

"It's all you, Sweet P," Candi said. "My money's on you."

For all I knew, Candi could have been betting money on me. As I walked to my spot on the field, Denise and I lined up back to back. It was whoever could rush down field and kick the ball into the goal the fastest. Coach Oslo and Rita each had a stop watch.

"Ready, set..." Rita called out. "GO!"

I charged ahead. I didn't need to calculate how many steps I needed before I took a shot. I just felt it. When the time was right, I wound up and blasted it. It was good. Rita blew her whistle.

"Big Time does it again!" she called out.

All my teammates cheered. Molly slapped Jules five. Angel patted Lucy on the back. Even Wil smiled and reached out her hand to Candi.

Once the celebration was over, we collected our prize. Two free pizzas. But before anyone could go away, Coach Oslo called out, "It's time for the coaches to play!"

Everyone gathered in the bleachers. I walked over and stood next to Kara.

"Do you wanna play in this?" I asked.

"Yeah," she replied. "Why not?"

"I think it's just us two and no other campers," I said.

Kara turned to me and her eyes grew wide. We both turned and waited for our instructions. Rita called out for everyone to quiet down.

"There's a player here who is always thinking about her teammates," Rita said. "She's always thinking about you. All of you. I want you to know that when I went to her about playing in this game, she asked if all of you could play, too. Does anyone know who I'm talking about?"

Everyone's eyes turned to me. Candi smacked me on the back. Molly smiled. Angel whispered, "Penny, it's you. It's gotta be you."

My face burned in embarrassment. *Why did Rita have to make such a fuss? Why did she have to single me out all the time?*

"Every cabin gets to play against us for two minutes," Rita said, and my heart stopped. *She actually listened to me!*

"And we're not keeping score. This is for fun. Just the way Penny Harris wants it."

Everyone started cheering.

"Yeah, P!" Jules said.

"Thanks, Penny!"

"Yeah! Thanks!"

I smiled. All the extra attention actually came in handy for once. Everyone was smiling, and having a good time. I thought for sure it was going to be the best night at camp.

Until what happened later that night.

Chapter Fourteen

The bats fluttered around in the dark sky above us.

"Bats freak me out," Candi said as we all walked up the hill to our cabins.

"They give me the creeps, too," Wil said.

"Last night I woke up and one was right above my face hanging upside down," Rosie told us.

"In the top bunk?" Molly replied.

"Yeah," Rosie said. "I almost screamed."

"I would have done more than scream," Wil said.

"I'd watch it, Rosie," Candi added cautiously. "You have all that hair and bats love hair."

"I've been wearing my baseball cap to bed every night," she said.

I laughed, thinking of how excited Rosie must have been knowing that we'd be heading back to Broadway in less than 24 hours.

"I can't wait to get home," Wil said. "I can only stand being in the woods for so long."

Everyone stopped on the porch of our cabin. For some reason, I still had a ton of energy. I didn't feel like going in just yet.

"I'm tired," Wil said. "I'm going to bed."

As she walked up the stairs and pulled open the creaking door, Angel followed right behind her. "Good night," Angel said.

"I got the first shower then," Molly said.

"I'm next," Rosie called out.

Kara and I stayed out on the porch with Candi, Jules and Lucy.

"How much time do we have before lights out?" Candi asked.

Jules bent over and tilted her watch under the light. "Twenty minutes," she said.

An awkward moment of stillness passed. The wind blew and a strange feeling swept over me as we were sitting there doing nothing.

"Let's do it!" Candi called out.

"Do what?" Kara asked.

"Sneak over to the boys' cabin!"

I immediately shook my head, and so did Kara.

"You two are no fun," Candi said. "Live a little, P. Do something wild for once. Nobody's gonna catch us. We'll run over and run right back."

I couldn't see Kara's face in the darkness, but I knew by her silence that she had to have been thinking the same as me. If Kara wanted to do it, I guess I could do it, too. I dropped my head down again.

"I'll do it if Kara does," I said.

Kara didn't say anything. It was as if I had made the decision for her. When Candi jumped up, everyone followed. As we moved down the dark path, my insides tightened, and my nerves tingled. I looked down to my feet and saw the white line in front of us, and held my breath as I ran over it. Jules tripped and everyone started giggling. Then we ran up to the boys' door and stopped. We formed a tight huddle together, and Candi started whispering.

"When you hear me whistle, everyone rush in," she said.

I crept around the side of the cabin, and moved cautiously through the darkness. All I could think of were animals and bugs and snakes. I stood on my tiptoes and peeked into the window. I heard the boys talking, and spotted the ray of a flashlight. Then I heard a whistle.

When Candi screamed wildly, my heart skipped a beat. Within seconds, Candi, Jules, and Lucy had ambushed the place. The boys almost jumped out of their sleeping bags. I started laughing and couldn't stop. I'd never heard boys scream so loud.

"You are gonna pay for this!" one boy yelled to Candi, who was laughing so hard she sounded like she was in pain.

Then I stopped suddenly, and glanced around nervously for counselors. I looked to my right. Then my left. My eyes stopped on the path back to Cabin F. Kara came up behind me, unlatched the hook on the door, and pushed me inside. When one boy flicked on the light, Candi shouted, "Turn it off! They'll see us."

Jules, Lucy, and Candi made themselves comfortable on the beds.

"What are we doing tonight?" Lucy asked.

Hold up. Time out. Had they been here before? I looked to Kara. She didn't say a word. She just watched in disbelief as Jules opened a pack of cigarettes. One of the boys slid a suitcase out from under his bed. He pulled out a can and tossed it to Kara. Instinctively, she reached out and caught it. When she turned it over, we both saw that it wasn't soda. It was beer. I glared at Kara to put the beer down. She set it on the sill behind her.

"Aren't you gonna drink that?" a boy asked Kara.

"Take a sip," Jules added. "Go ahead."

Then I heard a deep voice shout, "What's going on in there?"

I unhooked the latch and bolted out of that cabin so fast that I didn't even feel my feet touch the ground. The only noise I heard was the banging on the door I had closed behind me.

"Penny!" Kara yelled.

I whipped my head around. The lock had jammed and Kara was stuck. *What should I do?* My mind flashed to the beer, the cigarettes, and the boys. *What would my parents and my grandmother do if they heard about me being in the cabin? What about Mr. G? He would never trust me again.* No one would ever believe that I didn't want to go there in the first place. I turned back around and headed toward Cabin F.

As my feet pounded down the path, I heard a heavy breathing coming right at me. It grew louder and louder. I sidestepped behind a tree, and held my breath until the body passed. It was Coach Oslo. I could tell by the way he was running and grunting that he was mad. Really mad. After he passed, I tiptoed down the trail.

Finally, I reached Cabin F. I stopped not wanting to go inside until I caught my breath and pulled myself together. The front door creaked open, and the light from a flashlight struck me in the face.

"What are you doing, P?" Angel said. "Are you all right?"

"Yeah," I said. "I'm fine."

I walked by her and went straight to my bunk. Everyone sat up and watched me carefully as I took off my shoes and put on my bed clothes.

"Where were you?" Molly asked.

"Just hanging out," I answered as I wiped the sweat on my brow with my sleeve. The room fell silent.

"I'm gonna take a shower," I picked up my soap and towel. "Where's the flashlight?" I asked.

Angel handed it to me and I flicked the switch. Another awkward second passed. I could feel my friends looking at each other for some kind of explanation. *This wasn't me. What I did wasn't me.*

"Where's Kara?" Wil asked.

My eyes began to water, and a lump formed in my throat. I walked toward the shower unable to speak.

I had left Kara all by herself.

Chapter Fifteen

"Where is she?" Molly called out.

"I don't know," I mumbled from the bathroom.

I quickly turned the faucet and stepped inside. After a long shower, I took extra time in the bathroom putting on my clothes and brushing my teeth. I dreaded walking back into the bunks. *What if Kara was there? What if the Ballplayers found out?* I reached around with my hands and walked slowly through the darkness, careful not to trip over or bump into anything. No one stirred, which meant they all must have fallen asleep. I took another deep, quiet breath. I crawled into my bed and looked at Kara's mattress. It was empty. *What is taking so long? Where is she?*

"Penny," I heard a voice whisper.

I jumped and then turned to the bed next to me.

"What'd you do, Penny?" Angel asked.

"Nothin'," I replied.

"I won't tell anyone," she said. "Something's bugging you. I can tell."

I didn't say a word. I glanced nervously around the room. When no other bodies stirred, I turned back to Angel.

"We went to the boys' cabin," I admitted.

"You crossed the line?" Angel asked loudly.

"Shhh!" I said as I shifted my eyes about the room again. No one moved.

I turned back to Angel, and knew that I could trust her. After all, she helped me out with talking to Marvin. *But what would she think of me after I told her what I had done?* I was supposed to be the leader. *How could I mess up so bad?*

"What happened?" Angel asked. "You can't hold it all in. You've got to tell somebody."

I took a deep breath and began my story.

"They had cigarettes and beer," I whispered. "A counselor came to the front door. I ran out the back."

"What happened to Kara?" Angel asked.

"I don't know," I muttered in shame. "The door locked and she got stuck inside. I didn't know what to do. Mr. G would be so mad at me if I got caught. I shouldn't have done it. It was so stupid."

I wanted Angel to tell me that everything was OK, and that I did the right thing by leaving. But even she knew it wasn't that simple. Before Angel could say anything, the front door creaked open, and Kara walked in. I sat up in my bed. She didn't even look at me.

"What happened?" I asked her.

Silence. Dead silence.

"Are you OK?"

A stubborn, mad-as-heck silence jabbed me in the gut. Kara walked into the bathroom, and I laid back down in my bed. *What would I say next? Sorry? That I'd turn myself in? Could I do that? Should I say anything?*

Kara returned to the bunks, and slipped into her bed without a word.

"I'm sorry," I whispered. "I didn't mean it. I didn't know what to do."

Kara shut me out of her world. She didn't care about me anymore, just like the first day of camp when she didn't know me. Nothing I said could have undone what I did.

I never felt so low.

• • • •

When we woke up the next morning, Kara was gone.

"Where is she?" Molly asked. "Did she come in last night?"

"Yeah," I said.

"Something must be wrong," Wil added.

"You think the Hookman got her?" Rosie said.

Everyone laughed except me. I felt so guilty that I wanted to pack up my bags and go home. I didn't deserve to be at camp.

When we went to the cafeteria for breakfast, we passed Kara on the main field. Lucy and Candi stood behind her. Coach Oslo took a deep breath and blew into his whistle. Kara burst ahead. She pumped her arms and gritted her teeth as she ignored all the curious eyes that had fallen on her.

"What are they doing?" Wil asked.

I shrugged and my eyes fell to the ground. I belonged out there with Kara. I felt like a coward. A rotten, no-good coward.

Denise and Lisa walked over to us.

"Did you hear what they did last night?" Lisa said.

"What?" Wil asked.

"They were out drinking in the boys' cabin," she replied.

When everyone gasped, my blood boiled.

"Not Kara," I said. "She wouldn't do that."

"Uh-huh," Denise said.

"How do you know?" I asked.

"That's what I heard," Lisa said.

"Where's Jules?" Angel asked.

"I guess she got kicked out," Lisa said.

"She was sent home," Denise added. "And never allowed back. She was drinking."

It amazed me that Denise and Lisa let a story get so out of hand. Nothing they said made sense.

"If Jules got kicked out because she was drinking," I asked, "then how come the rest of them didn't?"Lisa looked at Denise. Denise looked at Lisa. They both shrugged. They didn't care. All they wanted to do was tell a story.

"You might want to mind your own business," I added.

They both shot me a dirty look, and then trudged away. Angel's wide eyes fell on me. Molly looked at me and asked, "What's wrong, Penny? You've been actin' weird."

"Nothin'," I replied. "I guess I'm just cranky and tired."

Wil eyed me suspiciously and said, "You're never cranky."

By the time we sat down to eat, every player in camp thought they knew what happened. One table was talking about how Candi had snuck over every night that week. Another said that they had heard Jules and Lucy talking about smoking all the time. Then one girl said, "Kara's such a..."

I stopped, turned, and locked my eyes into hers.

"Take it back," I called out firmly.

Her eyebrows raised as she glanced at me. "What?" she asked.

"Take what you said about Kara back," I said. "You don't even know her. How can you go talking about her like that?"

"It's true," the girl said. "She got caught."

Angel pushed me in the back, and said, "Come on, Penny. Let's go." I turned away and watched as Kara, Candi, and Lucy walked into the room. Everyone stared as Coach Oslo followed them through the food line. Kara kept her eyes on the ground. Lucy and Candi fidgeted and whispered things back and forth. They all sat down at a table in the corner with Coach Oslo.

"They're in *trouble*," Wil said. "Coach Oslo is ticked."

"How could they be so stupid?" Molly asked. No one replied. "I can see Candi, Jules, and Lucy doing it because they're crazy. But Kara?"

"I told you she was weird," Wil said.

My eyes shifted to Angel. I had to confess. I couldn't let this go any longer.

"Maybe Kara didn't want to go," Angel said. "There's no sense in us getting all over her case. She's got enough problems with Coach Oslo."

Angel's explanation quieted the group. I started wishing that the problem would just go away, but the public humiliation only became worse. After we finished our breakfast, we walked up to the return window and handed in our trays to the dishwasher. He passed everything back to Candi and Kara. Kara's pale blue eyes fell upon me and then she turned away quickly. Candi scowled at me.

"I can't believe they have to do dishes, too," Wil said. "I'd leave before I started washing dishes."

"Not if Mr. G found out you did something wrong," Molly said. "You'd do anything not to have him find out."

That was not what I wanted to hear. Molly was right. After all Mr. G had done to get us here, the worst thing in the world we could do was disappoint him.

Word couldn't get back to Mr. G.

• • • •

Before we started tournament play, we had one last round of stations to complete.

"What's up, Sweet P?" Rita asked as I jogged over with the rest of the players. "How many goals are you gonna score today? A dozen or more and I'll buy you an ice cream sandwich."

With all the things swirling around in my head, I didn't really care about kicking a soccer ball around at the moment. Kara was standing right next to me, and I couldn't bear to look at her. Rita blew the whistle and we hustled into line for the fast break drill. I looked up at the player who I had to mark. It was Kara.

"Come on, Penny!" Rita cheered. "Stay tough!"

The whistle shrieked, and we raced down the field. After five steps, I let Kara have the ball. Even with Rita cheering for me, giving the ball to Kara was my only way of apologizing for what I had done. In the next station, I could barely drag myself through the drills. When Coach Oslo and Rita started tearing into me about hustling, I ran harder, but Kara outplayed me on virtually every possession. And no matter how many incredible plays Kara made that day, Coach Oslo and Rita didn't say a word to support her. In their minds, she was trouble. At the end of the stations and drills, Kara went off by herself. I walked up the path with Rosie on my side.

"Are you all right?" Rosie asked.

Her pretty almond eyes looked up at me with great concern. I lifted my head up. Before I could answer, I spotted Lucy and Candi behind a tree.

"Hey, Penny!" Candi called out. Her muscles in her face were tight. Her brow furrowed. She glared at me as I walked over.

"Why'd you go leave us last night?" she asked.

Rosie's head turned to me. Her eyes begged me to say it wasn't true. I half-shrugged, and Rosie's shoulders drooped in disappointment. She had put it all together. I turned back to Candi. Her eyes turned angrier. "If it weren't for Kara," she said. "You'd be running and doing dishes with us."

I squinted at her and shook my head in confusion. "What?" I asked.

"Kara wouldn't rat on you," Lucy explained. "She refused to say you were in that cabin. No matter what we said, Coach Oslo didn't believe us when we told him you were there."

Candi added sarcastically, "Not Penny. Penny's perfect. She wouldn't do such a thing. I guess it's only people like us who get caught and actually get in trouble for it."

Candi moved closer to me, and Lucy pushed me on the shoulder. I didn't raise a hand. Just as they moved in on me, I heard footsteps and heavy breathing.

"Don't even think about touchin' her!" Molly threatened Candi.

Candi and Lucy scoffed at Molly.

"What are you, her personal bodyguard?" Candi said and she laughed at her.

Molly said nothing. She stood there, back straight, fists clenched, ready to get herself tangled up in a mess when she didn't know half the story.

"Let's go," I told Molly as I grabbed her arm. She tried wrestling away from me, but I didn't let go. We turned and walked away. Rosie followed right behind us.

"I guess Penny didn't tell you that she was with us last night," Candi yelled. "She was with us."

It was as if she had shot us all in the back. As our steps slowed, my heart sank.

"Yeah right," Molly muttered nervously. She didn't want to believe what she had just heard. But my best friend was no dummy. She knew I'd been acting strange. "You weren't there, were you, Penny?"

"Yeah," I muttered in shame. "I was."

There it was again. That I-can't-believe-Penny-would-do-such-a-thing silence. Molly needed a few seconds to piece it all together. I had to say something.

"I'm sorry," I said. "I never should have done it. It was stupid."

"What happened?" Rosie asked.

I breathed a sigh of relief. At least one person was willing to hear me out. I told them what happened.

When I was finished, Molly huffed and asked, "What are you gonna do?"

She knew what I had been struggling with. As much as it hurt her to find out that I'd snuck around and then kept the truth from her, she knew why I did it.

"Mr. Gordon will be really mad," she said and her eyes grew wide. "Really mad."

"I know," I muttered.

"What are you going to do?" Angel asked.

I shrugged and decided I needed more time to think about it. The whistle blew and we ran on to our field for our 11-on-11 tournament. During the entire game, Rita kept yelling, "Come on, Penny! Get your head in the game!" For the last few minutes, I played as hard as I could, and we won the game.

"Who do we play for the championship?" Denise called out after the game.

"The Twisters," Rita replied.

I sighed. I wasn't excited about playing in the championship for one reason.

We'd have to beat Kara's team in order to win.

Chapter Sixteen

As we walked down to the main field, a deep voice called out, "Penny, Molly, Wil!"

When we turned and spotted Mr. G, he looked at us and waved. I tried to smile, but my guilty eyes shifted away from him.

"Hi, Mr. G!" Molly said cheerfully.

"How's everything going?" he asked.

"Great," Wil replied.

"Any problems?"

Molly shook her head. "Heck, no, Mr. G.," she said with a wry smile. "Not us."

For a second, he raised his eyebrows suspiciously at Molly, and then he grinned. "That's what I like to hear," he added. "Now you girls hustle on out there and show me what you've learned this week. I'll be cheering."

"We're not playing," Molly groaned. "It's Rosie's and Penny's team against Wil's."

"We'll see who can bring the championship back to Broadway!" Mr. G said proudly.

I started to think of how disappointed my parents would be if they found out that I was hiding something from Mr. Gordon. I remembered back to the day before we left for camp when my father agreed to help Marvin. I gave him my word that I would never feel sorry for someone who breaks the rules. As I took one long look at our principal and friend, I felt my insides begin to crumble. *I can't lie to him. I have to tell him the truth.*

"What's the matter, Penny?" he asked.

The whistle shrieked, and Rita yelled, "Let's go, girls!"

My eyes shifted nervously up at Mr. Gordon. All my shame and worry rolled up into one big mess, and I blurted out, "I've got to tell you something."

"Come on, Penny!" Rita ordered. "Hustle up!"

I huffed in frustration and looked to the ground. I hoped Mr. Gordon would sense how important it was for me to get things out in the air at that moment.

"You can tell me after the game," Mr. Gordon said with a smile. "Hustle on out there and show 'em how the kids from Broadway play ball."

I rolled my eyes and jogged away feeling empty and helpless. When I picked my head up from staring into the grass, I met my inevitable match. Kara's cold blue eyes looked clear past me. I wanted to speak, but no words could explain how awful I felt. All I could think of was how she called out for me to help her, and I kept running. Then I imagined how hard it must have been for her to stand there and listen to all the wonderful things the coaches said about me after she knew I was the lucky one who got away. *Why didn't she tell them the truth?*

Once the whistle blew, Kara was all business. She grunted as she sprinted and dribbled fiercely around the field. The other players tried catching her, but she darted around them anyway. No one could touch her.

With Kara dominating their offense, Rita screamed at me to help our defense. I rushed across the field and moved in on Kara. We both banged shoulders, and the whistle shrieked. Coach Oslo's angry eyes locked into Kara, and he screamed, "Stop pushing!"

When I bumped Kara on the next play, Coach Oslo let it go without a single threat or glare. We crashed into each other again, and he screamed, "Watch your elbows, Kara!"

Without one single complaint or protest, Kara kept pressing forward. I didn't know how she found it in herself to ignore what was happening. Coach Oslo and Rita couldn't have made it any more obvious why they were cheering for me. Kara was the branded troublemaker. I was the innocent one with all the friends. Everyone wanted me to win. With these thoughts weighing down my mind, I let one ball pass me. After I let it go by, I bent over and grabbed my shorts. I wanted to walk off the field and sit in the van until we were on the road back to Broadway Ave.

I stood by myself for about 30 seconds. Then without a ball at her feet, Kara ran over to me. She came right up to my face, and yelled, "Would you cut it out and just play!"

I stood in shock as I looked into her fierce, competitive eyes. I realized right then that the only way Kara would even think of forgiving me is if I let it all go and just played ball. My motor started running, and I sprinted forward. On the next drive down field, Rosie kicked me the ball right in the middle, and I slammed it into the goal. The crowd cheered wildly as I ran back to the center of the field, but I knew I had no right to smile.

That was only the beginning. Five minutes later, Kara drove down the left side and dribbled right past our keeper for the score. When the ball fell gently into the net, only one person from the crowd cheered.

Candi called out, "Way to go, Kara!"

For some reason I turned to Candi and Lucy on the sideline. They shot a dirty look at me and started whispering. I looked away and pretended not to care. When Kara jogged back to the middle of the field, I said quietly, "Nice shot."

She kept her lips tightly pursed, and she continued to fix her eyes on something in the distance. When the action continued, we each took turns sprinting and maneuvering our way down the field, passing one defender after another. When I scored my second goal, the coaches, the fans, and the parents put their hands together and rooted wildly for me.

"They can't touch you, P!" Wil cheered.

But even with all my smooth moves, Kara kept coming back with more effort and better plays. On her next possession, Kara kicked an incredible pass to her teammate, who nailed the easy open shot.

As we jogged back to center field, Rita called out our strategy.

"Get the ball to middle!" she hollered. "You've got to get the ball to Penny!"

After the whistle blew, I weaved in and out, and back and forth around the field feeling more comfortable with every step I took. When I spotted Denise wide open on the sideline, I kicked her ball.

"Get it back to Penny!" Rita screamed from the sideline. "Wake up, Denise! Penny's open!"

Denise did as she was told. With the ball back at my feet, I drove down the center of the field, ran right

141

past Wil, and blasted a shot. It fell in the upper right hand corner, just out of the keeper's reach.

"That's three!" Molly announced to the crowd. "Count 'em. One, two, three. Three for P! Way to go Penny!"

I jogged humbly back to center field. Rosie ran up to me and gave me a high five. We were up 3-2 with five minutes left on the clock. When Kara got her foot on the next ball, I could tell by the look in her eyes that she had something to prove. The more tired we grew, the stronger she became. Candi and Lucy started cheering louder and louder from the sidelines. Kara was everywhere her teammates needed her to be. None of our defensive players could stop her.

"Cross!" one girl called out. "Cross it to Kara!"

"Mark your player!" Rita called. "Somebody mark Kara!"

But it was too late. After two quick passes, Kara pounded the ball into the net. She jabbed her fist in the air, and then coolly jogged back to center field.

A hush fell over the stunned crowd of campers.

"How much time is left?" Angel called out.

"Two minutes," the scorekeeper yelled.

It was my time to shine. I got the ball and dribbled it around, not wanting to let it go. But when two players ran up to me, I spotted Denise all alone on the wing. I kicked her the ball.

"Get it back to Penny!" Rita screamed in desperation.

But Denise didn't listen. Rita had driven her to the edge. By giving me so much hype, Rita had made Denise and the rest of my teammates feel like nothing. I watched nervously as Denise angrily moved forward. She tangled herself up with another player, tripped and lost the ball. The halfback booted it to Kara, and she was gone in a flash. She crossed the ball perfectly to her right wing player, who drilled a shot that landed in the upper left-hand corner of the net.

My heart sank, and the horn blew. The championship slipped out of our reach. I managed a faint smile as I went around and slapped the hands of every player on the other team. When I came in front of Kara, I stopped and stared into her eyes. I thought I'd see happiness and joy, but I found nothing but emptiness. She dropped her head as she walked off the field alone.

I wanted to run and hide, but I could not escape the disappointment that spread through me. As I walked off the field, I couldn't bring myself to look at Mr. G or my friends.

"Have a seat, girls!" Coach Oslo called out.

I dropped down to the ground and picked at the grass as the awards ceremony began. I glanced up and watched as Rita held out the trophies, and Coach Oslo called out the names of every player on Kara's team. Wil marched up proudly after Coach Oslo called out her name. She came back to us with a pearly smile and said, "Maybe this week wasn't that bad after all."

I felt the shame all over again. There I was, so caught up in what a disaster my week had been that I never even thought about anyone else. Wil pumped her trophy up into the sky.

"Nice job, Wil," I said. I flashed my first smile all afternoon as I reached out and slapped her five. Then I turned my attention back to Coach Oslo.

"The most valuable player at camp goes to the player who did the most for her team," Coach Oslo said.

I picked through the crowd and spotted Kara. She was easily the best choice as the most unselfish player and friend I'd ever met.

What? After I pieced together what was about to happen, my mind fluttered in a panic. *No! Not me!*

"The MVP goes to Penny Harris," Coach Oslo called out.

The crowd erupted in cheers. I turned to the Ballplayers and did not move.

"Come on up here, Penny!" Rita called out impatiently.

I pulled myself up off the ground. My eyes searched the crowd to find the person I had stolen the award from. After I looked past Candi's scowl and Lucy shaking her head in disgust, I found who I was looking for — Kara. I glanced up at Coach Oslo. My face turned hot, and my palms began to sweat.

"I can't take this," I told him.

Coach Oslo's brow furrowed. "Why not?" he asked.

"I won't take this," I stated firmly. "It belongs to Kara."

Chapter Seventeen

I looked around only to see all the smiles fade. As everyone waited for an explanation, I turned to the Ballplayers. Molly's deep blue eyes softened. Angel nodded her head slightly. Rosie shook her head, and Wil's mouth dropped open.

My eyes stared at the ground as I began to speak. "The only reason why Kara didn't get this award was because she got caught," I said.

I built up the nerve to turn to Kara. This time she didn't turn away. A chill shot up my spine.

"I was in the cabin, too," I admitted.

I glanced at Rita, who was standing right next to me. I could tell by her wide eyes that she didn't want to believe the truth about her favorite player. Neither did Coach Oslo. The silence hung in the air as I walked over to Kara and handed her the trophy. She didn't take it. Then I stuck it closer to her.

"It's yours," I said. "You're the best. Take it."

She slowly reached up her hand. I heard one person clap and then another. Within seconds, the entire camp had their hands together. As I sat back down right next to Kara, I made sure that I did not flash one of my nervous smiles to the crowd. Despite all the cheers, I had nothing to be proud of.

Once the crowd stopped clapping, I took a deep breath and glanced over at Mr. Gordon. He stared blankly at me and then nodded his head. I didn't know what to make of it. When I was standing in front of the crowd, I had forgotten all about what he would think or do. All I thought of was how I had to speak the truth for Kara, for my friends, and above all for myself.

I felt a jab in my side, and I looked up. It was Kara poking me with her trophy.

"Why do you always have to be so serious?" she said with a grin. "Are you ever going to talk to me again?"

In an instant, my sadness turned into a joy. I knew that instant that I finally had been forgiven.

When the announcements were over, Molly and Angel ran up to me and slung their arms over my shoulder. Wil and Rosie followed right behind.

"Hurry up!" Rosie said with a wide grin. "Let's get outta here!"

Everyone burst out laughing. But as we walked closer to Mr. G, my nerves tingled and my smile disappeared. He stopped right in front of me and waited for me to begin.

"I'm sorry for disappointing you," I mumbled.

He paused until I picked my head up and looked into his eyes. "I heard about the girls who snuck out that night," he said. "And I didn't want to think that any of my girls would do such a thing."

A lump formed in my throat, and I felt rotten all over again.

"After you did the wrong thing, you did the right thing by admitting you made a mistake," he said. "You're lucky you had a chance to make up for it."

I nodded my head and listened as Mr. G continued.

"I don't know what exactly you did, or what took place. What worries me is what could have happened. Do you understand that?"

"Yes," I said.

He put his arm around my shoulder, and I breathed a sigh of relief.

Within one minute, the Ballplayers, Kara, and I were in a full sprint to Cabin F. Rosie wasn't the only one who wanted to get back to the city.

"Who's going to the park when we get home?" Molly asked.

"I am," I said.

"I might take a nap first," Wil said. "Nah. I'll be there."

"I'll be down after dinner," Angel added.

Rosie didn't say anything, which meant she was going to stay put at the place she wanted to be all week. Home.

After we finished stuffing all our clothes into our bags, Kara and I swapped addresses and promised each other that we'd write. I looked up at her and told her one last thing before we parted.

"Thank you," I said sincerely, "for being a real friend."

She shrugged.

"Only a real friend would have done what you did for me," I added. "You didn't have to cover for me."

"I did it because I knew you never wanted to be there in the first place," she said. Then her eyes dropped to the ground. "Neither did I."

We all left Cabin F together, and lugged our bags down to the parking lot. I looked up and saw Candi and Lucy staring in our direction. I dropped my bag down and said to my friends, "I'll be right back."

Candi and Lucy looked at each other, muttered something and shook their heads as I walked up to them.

"I want to say I'm sorry for leaving you like that," I said firmly. "It wasn't fair to you either."

Candi's eyes remained lost in the distance.

"Is somebody talking?" she asked Lucy.

Lucy glanced quickly at me. For that split second, I thought I had a chance. Then she looked back at Candi and shrugged.

"Besides that one night," I said, "I had a lot of fun with you. I'm going to try and remember that."

I turned away and hoped they would find it in themselves to forgive me, but I accepted that I would never really know for sure. I joined my friends who had already started piling into the van.

Coach Oslo and Rita walked over and stuck their heads inside the van to say good-bye. When they didn't make a fuss over me, I thought that maybe they had learned that I was human, just like everyone else.

"See you next year!" Coach Oslo called out. "You're the best, Sweet P! You'll be big time someday."

He still didn't get it.

As we drove off, I stared out the window and tried to sort out everything that had happened that week. I knew I'd have to give the full report to my parents, which also meant some punishment would follow. But that wasn't what worried me.

All I could think about was how much it would hurt to tell my grandmother what I had done.

Chapter Eighteen

O nce we hit the open road, I leaned back in my seat and nodded off to sleep. When I felt an elbow push me in the side, I opened my eyes.

"Wake up, P," Molly said. "Wil's leaving."

What seemed like a few minutes of shut-eye turned out to be over an hour of heavy sleep. I looked up and recognized all the houses and cars of Broadway Ave.

"See you later," Wil called out.

I sat up in my seat, yelled good-bye and then waited for my stop. After Mr. Gordon pulled to the Jones' house, Rosie calmly stepped out of the car. She lifted her heavy bag over her shoulder.

"Thanks, Mr. G," she said quietly.

An excited grin crossed her face for a brief second, but she continued to keep her cool. As we drove off, Molly, Angel, and I turned over our shoulders and watched our little friend carefully. When Rosie dropped her bag on the porch and sprinted into her house, we all laughed aloud.

"It feels good to be home," Molly added with a sigh.

After Mr. G dropped off Molly, he stopped in front of my house. I yelled my good-bye and then trudged over to my steps. I could smell the sweet potato pie. The second I pushed open our front door, Sammy ran up to me and wrapped his arms around my waist. I patted him on the head and grinned. My grandmother came out of the kitchen and greeted me with a big smile.

"He's been waiting all day for you," she said.

Sammy picked up his head and asked, "Penny, can we go to the park?"

"Let me talk to Grandma for a second," I told my brother. "Will you take my bags into my room?"

He eagerly grabbed the strap of one of my overstuffed bags and started dragging it down the hallway.

"Where are Mom and Dad?" I asked.

"They're at a wedding," my grandmother replied. "They should be home in an hour or so."

For a brief second, I thought of waiting and telling all of them at the same time. Then I wondered if I could handle all three of them lecturing me at once.

"How many letters did you write me?" my grandmother asked.

I didn't respond.

"They should be delivered to my place within a couple of days," she continued. "I can't wait to read them."

I took a deep breath as I walked right past my grandmother and into the kitchen. She followed me in and asked, "Didn't you have fun at camp?"

When I shrugged, she didn't say another word. She pulled the chair out from under the table and sat down. I began my dreadful story. With her arms crossed on her chest, she listened without interruption. I could tell by her pensive stare that she was carefully watching every expression I made, and listening for the emotion behind my words. She always said she could tell if a person was speaking from her heart. I made my last apology, and then glanced up for some hint of what was going on in her mind.

"Do you remember what Reverend James said in church last week?"

I looked up at the ceiling and struggled to recall his exact words. "He told us something about character," I said.

"He said that character, not circumstance makes a person," she explained. "You put yourself in a very difficult situation. And you lost your character because you were afraid of what others would think."

I looked up and nodded again.

"Regardless of the circumstances," she added, "you need to stay true to yourself."

She paused so I wouldn't forget the lesson I had learned at soccer camp. We reached the end of the discussion when Sammy ran into the kitchen and asked loudly, "Can we go now?"

I looked to my grandmother, and waited for her decision. A few seconds passed. I hoped she would see that I had learned my lesson. *Please, please, let me go to the park!*

"Wait until your parents come home."

I had no idea how long that would be.

"Why can't she go?" Sammy asked.

I took another deep breath as I looked down at my happy little brother. His big eyes looked up at me and I shrugged. I did not want to tell him what a stupid thing I did.

"Go unpack your bags," my grandmother said.

As I started walking toward my bedroom, I felt Sammy's eyes on me. He wanted so badly to know what was going on. Everybody kept him in the dark about most matters because of his age, and he hated it.

"Come on, Sammy," I called out. "I'll tell you what happened."

Sammy raced past me and turned into my room. He picked up his speed, took off in the air and landed right on my bed. I lifted my bag off the floor and threw it on the bed next to him. I put together the most simple version of the story I could come up with.

"I had fun at camp," I said. "I met a lot of fun people. But one night we were just sitting around and one of the girls wanted to go to a part of camp where we weren't allowed. When I said I didn't want to go, some of the other girls said I was no fun. So I went."

"You did?" he gasped.

"Yeah," I said. "I didn't get caught, but everybody else did. All the other girls knew I was there, and they were mad because I didn't get caught."

"I'm glad you didn't," he said with relief.

I sighed as I looked at him.

"I did get caught," I said, "because I told the coaches what really happened."

"You did?" Sammy's eyes grew wide. "Why?"

"It was the right thing to do," I admitted. "It wasn't fair to the other girls."

Sammy's eyes turned toward my stereo and he started playing with the dial. That was the end of our conversation. I had no idea if anything I had said made any sense. The good thing was that it was over and done with. Well, almost over.

Then I heard the front door open. I walked into the living room and gave my parents a hug. When they both looked so happy to see me, I didn't think it would be appropriate to ruin the moment with my disappointing news. *Maybe I could wait a while.*

"Penny has a lot to tell you about camp," my grandmother told them.

My father's eyes fell on me. He could tell by his mother's tone something had happened. I plopped down on the couch.

I told myself that this would be the story to end all stories. I spoke clearly and humbly as I told them step-by-step what happened. When my parents interrupted me with their questions, I answered them calmly and told them that I knew what I did was wrong. After realizing there was nothing more to say, I just stopped talking and listened.

"You should have a higher standard for yourself," my mother said.

"I told her that," my grandmother said.

"I hope you learned your lesson," my father added.

"She'd better have," my mother groaned.

Then it turned into an open forum for discussion on life. They started calling out things to each other.

"Kids have to stay busy."

"Look at all the trouble out there."

"You have to be careful who you trust."

I raised my eyebrows and shrugged. They were right. *What more could I say or do?* The phone rang, and my father picked it up.

"Hi, Molly," my dad said. "Penny won't be at the park tonight. She has to stay in. She'll call you tomorrow."

So much for wishful thinking. I accepted my punishment and returned to my bedroom. I laid down on my bed and tried reading a magazine. But after one paragraph, my head rested into my pillow and I was down and out for the night.

● ● ● ●

After church the next day, I asked if I could go to the park. When I received the OK, I ran into my house and called up Molly.

"Meet me in five minutes," I said.

I hung up the phone and yelled for Sammy. He trotted into my room with his T-shirt in his hand and his shoelaces untied.

"Are we going now?" he asked.

"Yeah," I said. "Put your shirt on and tie your shoes."

I skipped down the steps and started dribbling my ball on the sidewalk. As my brother told me about all the things I missed at the park, I looked up and spotted Marvin standing in front of Old Man Miller's house. He reached down and pulled the string on a lawn mower. It didn't start. He tried it again. It didn't catch.

His eyes finally caught me staring at him. My nerves made me almost turn away. But I didn't. I couldn't. I was so glad to see Marvin working.

"Hi, Marvin," I said. "What are you doing?"

"I'm helping Mr. Miller clean up his place," he said.

"That's good," I added with a smile. "Are you going to go down to the park when you're finished?"

"I've still got to sweep the porch and water the shrubs," he said as he looked around.

As much as I knew that all the kids at the park would be betting on how long it would take before he would screw up and lose his job, I didn't care. All the words or wisdom and advice meant nothing compared to that moment. I had put it all together. Marvin and I had something in common. For as many people who expected me to do something good, there were that many people who expected him to do something bad. Nobody ever thought I could fail. Nobody ever thought Marvin could succeed.

I turned to my brother and said, "Go turn on the hose."

I bent over and picked up the broom that was lying on the sidewalk. An awkward moment of silence passed. I focused on the ground below me and hoped Marvin didn't think he had to apologize about the money. I didn't want him to think that I felt sorry for him. His eyes watched me carefully as I swept the dirt away.

"Did you have fun at camp?" he asked quietly.

"Yeah," I said. "Except for one night."

"What happened?" he asked.

"I did something I wasn't very proud of," I replied. "But it's over. I get to start again."

Marvin muttered, "I'm glad you got to go."

I looked up at him and felt butterflies flutter in my stomach.

"Thanks," I said with a smile. "I am, too."

About the Author

I am not very proud of this story, but I will tell it anyway.

When I was in fifth grade, I went to my first basketball camp. On the first day, I ran into the gym and started shooting. The director blew the whistle and we all sat down. I looked around and saw that I was one of three girls at a camp of almost 200 boys. At school, the boys didn't care that I played, so I assumed that my being a girl wouldn't be a big deal at camp either. But I was wrong. As I hustled through all the drills, the boys scoffed, snickered, and complained about every move I made.

When we split up into teams, my coach rooted for me and even set up special plays so I could score. Every time I did do something well, my coach cheered for me. But the boys continued to curse and glare at me.

On the third day, I woke up in the morning and decided that I didn't want to deal with the boys anymore. So I told my mother I didn't feel well, and I stayed home.

I sat out by the pool alone for hours that day with a rotten, empty feeling inside of me. The more I thought about what I did, the worse I felt. I realized that staying home hurt me more than anything the boys said or did.

After convincing myself that I just took a day off, I went back to camp the next morning. I went to look for my coach to tell him I was back, but I found out that he had to leave camp early. A short boy who had been picked on by the other boys just like me, came up and said, "Your coach said that you quit."

His words hurt me because he was right. I did quit. I was so wrapped up in all the people who didn't believe in me, that I forgot about the one person who did.

I can still recall all the things I felt that week at camp. In the past few months, I've had to make some big decisions about my company and this series of books. Everyday I have my family, friends and kids telling me how much they believe in me. Those are the only people I hear.

In your hands is my third book.

Be on the lookout for more books by

Broadway Ballplayers

Book #4
Don't Stop
by Angel

Angel Russomano loves to run and play. In high school, the cross country season and the soccer season are in the fall, so Angel decides to play on both teams. But the true test for Angel is balancing her sports with the pressures at school and problems at home. Will Angel be strong enough?

Due out in Fall '98

Book #5
Sideline Blues
by Wil

Back in third and fourth grade, Wil Thomas was one of the best athletes in her class, but now all of her teammates have caught up with her. Even though Wil tries her best, she is seeing less playing time in her volleyball and basketball games. Some teachers tell Wil not worry about sports and to concentrate on school, but she wants to play. What is Wil going to do?

Due out in Fall '98

Be a Ballplayer, too!